The Spy of Seoul: Escap
by
David Holmes

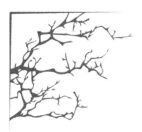

Chapter 1

"TAKE YOUR HANDS OFF me!" the young woman said in fluent English.

The conservatively-dressed middle-aged man gripped the girl's right arm more securely, guided her away from Seoul's War Memorial. "You are Park Jin Sun, correct?"

"If you know who I am, you should let me go."

The man tugged her toward the Han River. "You have dual citizenship, America and South Korea?" he asked in heavily-accented English.

"My friends call me Lisa." She pulled free of her involuntary escort. "But you are not my friend."

"No, I am not a friend."

She spun to face him. Eye to eye, they were the same height, about 5'9". He was on the stocky side, with gray hairs appearing at his temples, while she was slender with stylishly-cut black hair that framed an oval face. Her dark eyes looked larger than her contemporaries—a notable physical characteristic achieved without the cosmetic surgery nearly half of young Korean women submitted to. There was the sound of boats on the river, horns blaring as they navigated the busy waterway of Seoul under the many bridges carrying traffic into the sprawling capital's central district. A mild June breeze blew over the street, rustling leaves on the tree-lined thoroughfare. A glance beyond the city's modern skyscrapers revealed dark storm clouds gathering above the mountains in the northeast. It was the season of the monsoon in Korea, the wind bringing rain off the Pacific. People passed around them, carrying umbrellas. The man noticed the girl's well-worn jeans, bright red cotton sweater and light hiking boots. She took note of his gray business suit, white shirt and navy blue tie...and black, highly-polished leather lace-up shoes.

"Are you the police?" she asked.

He shook his head. "Worse."

"KCIA?"

"I just want to talk to you, Jin Sun. There is a restaurant nearby. Are you hungry?"

She shrugged. "A glass of tea would be fine."

"This way," he said, and ushered her into a modern restaurant filled with businessmen sitting on mats or pillows at low tables, grilling their portions of meat.

She stepped back. "Dog meat. They're cooking dogs."

"They serve very good tea here."

"I have a dog."

"I understand. It is the American half of you speaking." He turned around and led her outside onto the sidewalk. "I am sorry to offend you, Jin Sun. There is a tea house on the next block."

Finally, seated at a low table in a traditional tea house, he explained, "You are not in any trouble. When I learned you had returned from America, I decided it was time."

She sipped the hot tea, put down the cup. "Time for what?"

He looked away, worry lines on his forehead.

"You're not arresting me or abducting me?" The hint of a smile played at her lips.

He lifted his cup, swiveled it a few times to cool the liquid. "I have no daughter, Jin Sun. My approach was clumsy."

She almost felt sorry for him, his discomfort so obvious. "What do you want?"

Other than the server, the place was empty. "Your name is Park Jin Sun. You were born in Seoul nineteen years ago. You achieved high scores on the KSAT the year you finished high school. As a result, you were admitted to Seoul National University. Your future was secure, full of promise. A high paying job on graduation with a *chaebol*—Samsung, Hyundai, LG, take your pick—and an equally privileged marriage. Instead, you travelled to America and enrolled at UC Berkeley. May I ask why?"

"You know so much about me. I know nothing of you."

"I am known as Roh Dae-Jung. Please call me Roh."

"That is not your real name, I think." Again, that half-smile.

"Is that important?"

"Perhaps. Perhaps not." She drank more tea. The sound of cars and trucks honking intruded from the street. The siren of an emergency vehicle grew louder. "Like other students, I studied hard to ace the college entrance exam. 'Sleep five hours and fail, sleep four hours and pass.' That's what we all said. And it's true. I sacrificed time with family and friends for my education, to honor my parents."

"Your mother makes a very good living with her private tuition company."

"Yes, many families spend up to one thousand U.S. dollars a month to pay for private lessons. They sacrifice much for their children, so much so that most parents can afford only one child."

"That isn't why you left Korea."

She set down the cup, chewed on a fingernail. "You know all about me, so you know what happened to my father."

The man lowered his gaze, spoke in a whisper. "Warrant Officer Park was my friend."

"I don't understand, Mr. Roh. He never mentioned you."

"Just Roh, please. Keep it informal, like in the U.S." He sighed again. "Wesley Park and I served side-by-side near the DMZ. We both flew helicopters along the demilitarized zone, engaged in active reconnaissance—he with the U.S. Army, and I with the ROK Army."

"Dad always had high praise for the troops of the Republic of Korea."

"I was flying the day his chopper went down inside the zone."

She sat up straight, said quietly, "The army told mother it was an accident, a mechanical failure."

Roh shook his head. "You must know the truth, Jin Sun, however painful. It is your right to know."

"What do you mean?"

"Your father was piloting his helicopter close to the DMZ, but had not crossed into it. I know that because I was aloft half-a-mile west of the incident."

She dropped the tea cup on the floor, didn't pick it up. "Incident? You're saying it wasn't an accident?"

"His chopper was shot down."

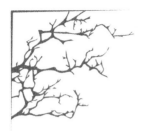

Chapter 2

HER HAND WENT TO HER mouth, tears appeared in her eyes. "Oh, my...my God," she choked out. "Are you sure?"

"I saw tracers coming from north of the DMZ."

"You reported it?"

"Of course." He shrugged. "No one wanted the truth to get out. They feared a crisis on top of the ongoing tensions over Pyongyang's missile launches. I submitted a formal report, but it was filed away, no action taken on it. I was transferred to the KCIA, a liaison position with the army. In effect, they are keeping an eye on me. As your father once said about the service, 'Don't rock the boat.'"

"It happened three years ago. Why tell me now?"

"Recently I learned—it was a misrouted paper—that my agency had investigated the incident in cooperation with the American CIA. The officer in charge of the unit that fired on your father's aircraft was none other than a Captain Pak Sung."

"So?"

"The son of Pak Chul, once an officer in the North Korean Army. In 1976, Pak Chul was a lieutenant along the DMZ. He confronted a U.S. Army work detail that was trimming foliage from a poplar tree in the DMZ, clearing limbs that obstructed the view between two United Nations' checkpoints. Pak Chul insisted that the Americans stop work and leave the zone. The U.S. Army major leading the detail refused. Pak Chul called up reinforcements and became aggressive, felling the major with a karate chop to the neck. Then Pak's troops, armed with axe handles and iron pipes, bludgeoned the major and his next-in-command to

death, in addition to wounding several enlisted men." Roh got to his
feet. On the sidewalk, he said, "I have a plan."

After listening to what he had in mind, she blurted, "Revenge?"

Students wearing the familiar school uniforms of navy blue skirts,
white shirts and ties, for girls; the boys in black pants and jackets, white
shirts and red ties, surged around them on their way to private lessons
or study sessions after school. Many adult women wore the traditional
hanbok, consisting of a long loose gown known as a *chima*, some adding
a short jacket. The clothing was very colorful. Made of cotton or silk,
many were brilliant red, yellow or blue. The result was a welcome splash
of color and style added to the usual Western business outfits found
in any modern city, including South Korea's center of industry, finance
and government.

"Not on Pak Chul's son, unfortunately. Singling out a serving officer of the Korean People's Army is, practically-speaking, impossible."

"Then?"

"The father, Pak Chul, that cold-blooded murderer, is a senior ad-
visor to North Korea's leader, Kim Jong-Un. Believe it or not, he is vul-
nerable."

"He is still alive?" she said doubtfully.

"As American's like to say, 'As seen on TV.' We spotted him in
the background during last year's military parade through Pyongyang's
Kim Il-Sung square. We verified it was the same Pak Chul."

"He must be old now."

"In his 60s, apparently in good health."

"Why are you telling me this?"

Roh stepped off the curb and waved down a taxi. "I thought you
might be interested."

"Mother should know, too."

"Let me break the news."

She had a quizzical look on her face. "That's it then?"

"Go home. Think about what I have said."

She came to the curb. "I've done nothing but think and study for sixteen years. I want to *do* something."

"Your American side is coming through again." He got into the vehicle, lowered the window and passed her a business card. "As a matter of fact, I *am* looking for a volunteer. Think about *that*."

The taxi accelerated, leaving Park Jin Sun, aka Lisa, alone on the busy sidewalk. Thoughts swirled through her mind as she headed for the subway and her mother's apartment on the south side of the Han River, near the campus of Seoul National University. Her father's death had been a great shock which she had not come to terms with. The pressure to continue the long hours of study—sixteen hours a day, including class time—while her heart was broken, had taken a toll. Instead of staying in Seoul, she had gone to California to attend college. In South Korea now, what could a nineteen-year-old girl do to avenge a father's death?

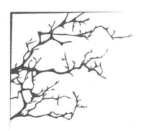

Chapter 3

PASSENGERS DISGORGED from the subway train, a blur of moving humanity pushing forward until, suddenly, time seemed to stop. Alone on the platform as the train's doors opened, a thin young man was holding up a long, folded black umbrella. Without speaking a word, he poked its metal tip into the neck of a distinguished-looking gentleman in a dark blue suit who had just stepped off the train. The older man immediately crumpled and fell headfirst onto the unforgiving platform. A split second later people were shouting and screaming, a kind of panic taking hold. As a uniformed policeman reached the scene the voices slowly subsided into an eerie silence.

Lisa kept her eyes on the umbrella man as he pushed through the crowd, away from the policeman. She followed him out of the subway station and watched him climb onto a motorcycle, the umbrella tucked under an arm. Before the license plate was blocked by unknowing pedestrians she caught sight of it. Then the bike with the attacker riding pillion disappeared into traffic heading north on the Banpo Bridge over the Han River.

"You there, in the red sweater," a man called out in Korean, "don't move!"

Lisa turned around and saw the policeman from the subway walking toward her. Emergency vehicles had arrived and paramedics and uniformed cops were entering the station.

"You are talking to me?" she asked.

"I remember your sweater. You saw what happened down there." The young police officer pulled out a small notebook and pen. "You are a witness. Tell me exactly what you saw."

"There are a lot of witnesses."

"It is your duty to report a crime."

"Is the man—?"

"Dead? Yes, and it was not a heart attack. He was killed." The policeman gestured with his pen toward the river. "The man with an umbrella fled the scene, climbed on a motorcycle. Describe him."

She did her best, finishing with, "He had a scar on his left cheek."

"Details?"

"About two inches long, apart from his mouth and eyes. Like this," she ran a fingertip along her cheek. "Why would anyone want to kill that man in the subway?"

"It is under investigation."

"Who kills with an umbrella?"

He stared at her directly. "Best not to speculate. Can you remember anything else?"

"Sorry. It happened so fast."

"You should not have followed the suspect. Did he spot you?"

"I don't think so."

He handed her the notebook and his pen. "Write down your name, address and phone number. A detective might want to get in touch with you."

She did as ordered, gave back the notebook. "I hope you catch him."

The cop took the pen from her hand. "I shouldn't speak of this, but it was probably political. We've had other incidents of North Korean agents active in Seoul. Usually it doesn't make the news, if you get my meaning."

Lisa nodded, the reality of what had just happened sinking in. "I won't talk to the media."

"If you think of anything else, call this number," he said, and handed her an official card.

She nodded again as he spun on his heels and went to a police car. Who was the victim? she wondered. Why was he killed? But she had no answers and trudged along with a heavy heart to her mother's apartment.

The small three-bedroom, two-bath apartment was on the 7th floor of a high rise, facing north to the modern skyscrapers of Seoul. She heard her mother in the kitchen, chopping vegetables—cucumbers, cabbage, eggplant and radishes, adding red peppers, ginger and garlic with a dash of salt. The result would be homemade *kimchi* that would go into a special small refrigerator in the kitchen, one made to mimic the traditional method of storing pickled vegetables in a ceramic pot underground in order to facilitate the fermenting process.

Leaving her boots at the door, Lisa slipped soundlessly inside the combined dining and living room and leaned against the open doorway to the kitchen, watching the food preparation. Since her father died, Lisa considered her mother her best friend and confidant. Mrs. Park was also the smartest person Lisa knew. Fluent in Korean, Mandarin, Japanese and English, her mother operated a thriving after-school tutoring business. Mrs. Park Eun-Joo, the latter names meaning 'Silver pearl,' was already an accomplished linguist, a graduate of the prestigious Yonsei University, when she had met and married a Korean-American Warrant Officer, Wesley Park, U.S. Army.

Lisa's grandfather had been a major in the army of the Republic of Korea, fighting alongside American troops in Vietnam. After that conflict, Major Park had moved to California, married a Korean woman in Los Angeles, who had given birth to her father. So, in fact, Lisa Park was of full-blooded Korean stock, though her father had been born and educated in America. His multiple postings to the Korean peninsula reflected not only his heritage and fluency in the Korean language, but also his suitability for sensitive assignments. Lisa assumed that that was how her father had come to know Mr. Roh.

"Lisa, you're home," her mother said, a bright smile lighting her delicate features. She was dressed in a red cotton *chima,* her hair still jet black, the very picture of a beautiful Korean housewife. "How was your first day back home?"

She stuffed her hands into the back pockets of her jeans, debating how much to reveal of her strange adventures. "Interesting, very interesting."

"Wash your hands, then rinse off the rice," Mrs. Park directed.

Lisa glanced at her mother. Such an intelligent woman, yet so dedicated to preparing a meal, she thought. How did she achieve this balance in her life?

"You are very thoughtful, my daughter. What are you thinking?"

"Mother, how did daddy die?"

Mrs. Park dropped her slicing knife, looked at her daughter. "Just what we were told by officials. Why do you ask now?"

She had assured Mr. Roh that she wouldn't repeat his story. A half-truth then. "I saw a man killed today...in the subway."

"Oh, child," her mother said, wiped her hands carefully on a dish towel and put an arm over Lisa's shoulders. "When was this?"

"Half-an-hour ago. A young man stabbed an older man with the point of an umbrella. The businessman went down, did not get up. The first policeman on the scene knew I had witnessed it and asked me questions."

"Could you identify the assailant?"

Lisa nodded. "Maybe, if I see him again."

Mrs. Park took the kettle off the stove, made a cup of hot tea and said, "Go to your room and rest. I will finish here."

Lisa turned and kissed her mother. She felt safe at home, a refuge from a hard, sometimes, brutal world.

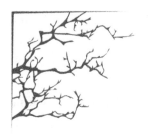

Chapter 4

LYING ON HER BED, LISA reached up to her bookshelf and brought down a volume on Korean history, determined to lose herself in the past if only for a short while. However, the history of her country was not that far different than the present; that is to say, life on the peninsula between China and Japan has long been characterized by a struggle to gain independence and keep that state of affairs.

Lisa shared her mother's talent for languages, having mastered the difficult Chinese alphabet with its many characters, and was able to read, write and speak like an educated member of that country. Additionally, she spoke very good Japanese though, like most Koreans, she harbored resentment for the harsh treatment of her country and people during the period of Japanese occupation between 1910 and 1945, when Korea was a virtual colony of that rising Pacific power. Yet, by the oddest of circumstances, her roommate and best friend at Berkeley was a Japanese-American student named Katy Kimura.

Of course, it was her facility in Korean and English that served her well in South Korea and America. While her mother made a good living teaching Korean, English and Chinese, the daughter had studied East Asian history at Berkeley, with the intention of obtaining a Ph.D in that field.

Flipping through the pages of the history book, she skipped the earliest period of human presence on the peninsula, dating back thousands of years before Christ. It was the century before the Nazarene trod the dirt roads of ancient Israel that Korea's culture began to form into what it was today. Three kingdoms strove for supremacy, a time when Confucius' teaching had great impact on the upper class and

Buddhism spread throughout the land in direct competition with shamanism for religious influence. At the end of the 14th century, a Korean general consolidated power, and thus began the Choson dynasty. The capital was established near the present city of Seoul and, significantly, one of the earliest kings of the dynasty oversaw the formation of a Korean alphabet, a simpler form of writing than Chinese that was also elegant in construction.

The Choson dynasty was particularly enduring, lasting from 1392 to 1910, the year Japan conquered the peninsular nation. Koreans had fought off Japanese and Chinese invaders over the centuries but the 20th century proved especially difficult. During the first half of the last century the land was stripped of most of its forest cover by the Japanese, the people were forced to learn and speak only Japanese in public and in schools, businesses and government. After the Japanese Imperial army invaded China's province of Manchuria in the mid-1930s, the next ten years was a period of constant warfare.

The final insult levied against the Korean people's dignity and respect was the practice of drafting young Korean women to work as 'comfort women' in brothels for the pleasure of Japanese soldiers. Such bad treatment by Japan was forgotten in Seoul, Pusan or any of the country's cities, towns and villages. As Lisa gazed at a map of her country, she noted the Yellow Sea on the west coast and the East Sea on the coast opposite Japan, not the Sea of Japan as that passage of water was on most international maps. Koreans referred to that body of water as the East Sea.

The latter half of the 20th century was remarkable for Korea as the country found itself divided, north and south, roughly at the 38th parallel. After WWII, the Soviet Union, an ally of the USA and Great Britain during that war, occupied the northern half of the peninsula while American troops held the south. 1948 was a momentous year on the international scene, featuring the reestablishment of Israel as a nation, freedom for India and, for South Korea, a newly-elected president and self-determination.

Unfortunately, the young nation had little time to develop before the new leader of the north—backed by Communist China, an ancient land where the communist army of Mao Tse-tung had defeated the Nationalist Chinese army after a long civil war that ended, also, in 1948—sent his Korean People's Army south of the 38th parallel and drove the ROK army and American units down to the southern tip of the peninsula. America's President Harry Truman sent famed WWII General Douglas MacArthur from Japan with additional troops, and soon the communists were pushed back beyond Seoul, all the way to the Yalu River and the border with China.

So-called Chinese volunteers, actually divisions of the People's Liberation Army of China, launched a fierce counter-attack that sent the Korean and American forces back toward Seoul. The United Nations sided with South Korea against the communist Kim Il-Sung's North Korea, many nations contributing troops and supplies for the defense of the south. The war then dragged on for two more years before an armistice was agreed to, though a peace treaty was never signed. The end of the shooting war institutionalized the separation of the Korean people, a demilitarized zone (DMZ) the most obvious physical barrier.

Lisa closed the book, lowered it to the floor. In modern history, she thought, only the division of Germany into a western-oriented half supported by the American, French and British military, and an eastern part dominated by the forces of the Soviet Union's Red Army bore any resemblance to her land's plight. East Germany had finally merged with West Germany after the fall of the Berlin Wall in 1990. But the Korean people still suffered the pain of separation. The literal breaking apart of families was diminishing with the passing of so many of the older generation, though many South Koreans still had relatives in the north.

After the deaths of Kim Il-Sung, the "Great Leader" and his son, Kim Jong-Il, known as the "Dear Leader," the enigmatic and increasingly erratic grandson of the North Korean political dynasty, Kim Jong-Un, seemed more determined then ever to turn his isolated country into a nuclear power...though not to supply his poor land with electricity; rather it was a means to blackmail other nations with nuclear weapons. The possibility of all-out war on the Korean peninsula appeared closer than at any time since the early 1950s.

"Jin Sun," her mother called, "supper is ready."

"Coming, mother," she said, and got up from her bed. She stared at a color photograph of her parents taken four years ago during the Harvest Moon Festival. Her mother wore her finest *hanbok,* a *chima* of yellow satin, her father wearing his Class A army uniform. Leaning on one another, both were smiling. Happier days, Lisa remembered wistfully.

Checking herself in a handheld mirror, she noted her Korean features, only the larger-than-normal eyes hinting at another influence. Though her father was raised in California, her grandparents on his side had both come from Seoul. It was her mind and attitude that reflected her Western background. Her mother had summarized her as a "Perfect Blend of East and West, the hope of the future. As she set down the mirror on her desk by the computer, she considered the latest news about her country's security predicament.

"Child, the food is getting cold," her mother said from the kitchen.

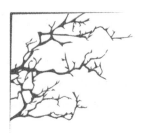

Chapter 5

THE ABSENCE OF HER father at the low wooden table was like a living thing, a familiar presence that had been abruptly taken away. Lisa knew it was hard for her mother to adapt to the loss of her husband, though Mrs. Park worked diligently at continuing family traditions. Although it would have been easier to simply eat a small meal in the kitchen, Lisa's mother insisted on placing bowls of white rice, a bowl of soup and, of course, *kimchi* on the table. Oddly, for a Korean, Lisa was not very fond of garlic; as a result, her mother used it sparingly. The girl's favorite spices and seasonings included ginger, small red peppers, and sesame seeds. She expertly used her chopsticks to spear vegetables, using the rounded spoon for eating the rice. In accordance with Korean custom, little was said during the meal. Concentration was saved for savoring the flavors and texture of the food. Afterward, she helped her mother clean up.

"When will Heidi return?" she asked.

Mrs. Park glanced at the open door of the crate, at the soft cushion inside it. "Mrs. Yong now walks five dogs from this building. It takes awhile to clean up after them, before bringing them back."

"Do older citizens still stare disapprovingly at her?"

"Don't worry. There is one species favored for its meat. Dachshunds enjoy an exempt status." She smiled radiantly. "You should not be too hard on older folks. It is an ancient custom, hard to abandon."

"I will go down and meet our dog-walker. By the way, how did Mrs. Yong stumble onto the job?"

"Remember her visit two years ago to see her son in San Francisco? She learned of dog-walking there."

"Be back soon," Lisa said and, skipping the elevator, went down the stairs to the ground floor. Once outside, she spotted Mrs. Yong and her leashed charges near the university's campus. As one of the dogs was doing its business, the dog-walker pulled a green plastic bag from a tan canvas holdall hanging from her right shoulder. That's when a boy wearing jeans and a black vest ran from a line of trees, over the grass and around the dogs. The animals began barking and running around, entangling Mrs. Yong in the leashes until she tumbled onto the grass. The boy stopped as if to help her up, then grabbed the canvas bag by its fabric handles and pulled it off her arm.

From fifty yards away, Lisa heard him shouting, "Let go of the leash handles or I will break your hand." Reluctantly, Mrs. Yong complied and the boy pulled the bag free and ran across the field.

Lisa sprinted up to the woman. "Are you hurt?"

"He stole my purse!"

"Stay with the animals. I'll get it back for you."

The boy looked over his shoulder once and stumbled, then took off again. But Lisa Park was not only a top student. She liked to run and had kept in shape in Berkeley with long runs in the rolling hills above the campus, the land covered with dry, golden grass, the roads lined with eucalyptus trees. Before the boy reached the stand of trees, she caught up and tackled him.

He kicked himself free, got up and swung the bag at her head, but she ducked under it and upended him with a gracefully-executed leg sweeping move. She noticed a colorful dragon tattoo on his left arm as he pushed himself to his feet and tried a straight-arm punch at her mouth. She blocked it with her right arm, leaned back and kicked him hard in the stomach. The young thief went down, rolled over and threw the bag at her, which she plucked from the air.

"My friends will get you for this!" he gasped in Korean.

Taking deep breaths, she tried to calm herself down. "Only a stupid man marks himself," she said, gesturing at his left arm. "Easy for the cops to find you."

The boy pointed at the spot where he had attempted to steal the purse. "The dogs are getting away."

Instinctively, Lisa looked back. The dogs had gathered around Mrs. Yong. The boy's lie gave him time to get up and run away. "So," she said aloud, "maybe not too stupid after all."

By the time she reached the dog-walker a police car was at the curb, an officer taking the assaulted woman's statement. Lisa added her description, then gathered up the leashes and led the dogs to the apartment with Mrs. Yong. The woman's knees were scraped but not bleeding, her long skirt soiled with grass stains.

"Has this happened before?" Lisa asked.

"No. This has been a safe district. The policeman said the theft in daylight was unusual."

"Maybe related to illegal drug use."

"I don't know. I hope not."

"You must go to my apartment first, mother will want to treat your lacerations. I will deliver the dogs to their masters."

Inside the lobby, Mrs. Yong said, "I saw what you did to him. You are very brave, but you should let the police go after criminals."

"I had to take action. It's who I am."

The older woman nodded. "Your father would be proud of you."

"He made sure I studied Taekwondo, not just book learning."

Leaving Mrs. Yong at the elevator, Lisa lifted up her short-legged dog and took the other animals up the flights of stairs to their respective floors. Lastly, she carried Heidi up two more flights to the 7th, rubbing the brown short-haired dachshund's long back. "I missed you every day I was gone, Heidi-girl. Did you miss me?"

The dog seemed to understand and licked her face.

"Good dog. You're my best friend." Not that Lisa hadn't any human friends, but the years of rigorous study common among her classmates left very little time for activities together. Neither had she ever had a boyfriend. No time for that either, not for her or any of the boys her age. At Berkeley, she had maintained her disciplined habits, not tempted by the young romances sprouting up around her. She believed the time would come to meet the right person.

But that time was not now.

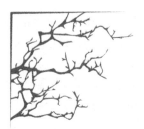

Chapter 6

HER MOTHER WAS BOTH horrified and proud of her daughter. "Just like your father," she said solemnly, "always ready to help someone in need."

Was this the right time to explain what she had learned about her dad's death? she asked herself. Although she had agreed to leave the talking to Mr. Roh, it felt like it was her duty to break the news. After her mother had cleaned Mrs. Yong's knees and hands with soap and warm water, patted down the broken skin with isopropyl alcohol, she accompanied her neighbor back to the woman's apartment. Back at her own place, Lisa went to the kitchen.

"Mother," she held out a hot cup of tea, "I have something to tell you."

Mrs. Park took the tea. "Please, tell me what is on your mind."

"I met a man today."

"Ah!"

"No, not like that." They conversed in English, as they often did at home. "He was about daddy's age. In fact, he introduced himself as a longtime friend."

"His name?"

"He called himself Roh Dae-Jung. I don't think that is his real name."

Still frowning. "Why would he lie?"

"*Kibun.*"

"He would lose face by revealing his true identity? I don't understand."

"He told a little white lie, that's all. The thing is, I believe him."

Her mother sipped the tea, nodded. "All right then, what did he say?"

Once again, Lisa took deep breaths to steady herself. "Daddy was killed."

"We know that. Killed in a helicopter accident while on joint maneuvers with our Korean Army near the DMZ."

Standing five inches taller, Lisa rested her hands on her mother's shoulders. "Mr. Roh said father's aircraft was shot down."

Mrs. Park's grip on the cup loosened. The glazed ceramic cup crashed onto the floor, splashing tea on their feet. Lisa reached for a kitchen towel, bent down and wiped up the spilled liquid, then collected the broken pieces of the cup. Her mother leaned over the sink and began to cry.

"I know it's a shock," Lisa said softly. "I can't stop thinking about it."

"Why did the government lie to us? Why did both the Korean *and* American officials deceive us?"

"I'm not sure," Lisa confessed. "Maybe it was to prevent a demand for retaliation against the North's new hotheaded young leader. That would make sense. Still, the authorities were untruthful."

Her mother turned around, wiping her eyes with a handkerchief. "We are his family. They should have told us the truth."

Should she mention that the name of the murderer had been revealed to her? No, her mother's heart was bruised enough. And it would serve no useful purpose. Then her phone vibrated in her pocket. She took it out and checked the number. Not the number of a friend, but a familiar number nonetheless. She reached into her other front pocket and drew out one of the cards given to her earlier. So, Roh was trying to contact her. Not surprising that he would have her number. He seemed to know so much already.

"Mother, will you be okay?"

"All the tutors are available today, the classes are covered. I wanted free time to spend with you."

"I have to go out again, just for a little while. Do your mind very much?"

Her mother managed a thin smile. "Be careful, Jin Sun. You're all I have now."

"I love you, mother." Lisa held her tight for a moment. "Don't forget to feed Heidi."

"Sometimes I think that little dog eats better than us."

Lisa laughed. "I'll be home early this evening."

"Wear a jacket over your sweater. And bring an umbrella."

Sure enough, mother was right. As Lisa stepped from the lobby, rain started falling, lightly at first, then heavy drops bounced off the pavement. Even the umbrella failed to offer complete protection. And that got Lisa thinking of the man in the subway, executed by the tip of an umbrella—a common object used to deliver a death sentence. What would happen next?

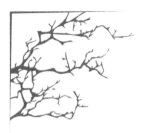

Chapter 7

IN THE MIDST OF THE mechanical noises of the subway station she called the number on the card. No answer so she left a message. She purchased a ticket and descended to the platform, boarded a train north into central Seoul and took a seat. Her folded umbrella left a puddle at her feet. She looked around at her fellow riders. Men and women, high school and university students, all seemed like normal human beings. Yet that's how she'd felt heading south on the same line just hours ago and a man's existence had been terminated. Quickly her world had become a very different place.

Then her phone rang, breaking through her morose thoughts. "Lisa here," she answered and heard a friendly voice. "Sally! How are you?" Sally Chu, her best friend in this world, aside from her mother; not a Korean citizen, but a permanent resident from Taiwan. South Korea was one of the most homogeneous societies on the planet. Few foreigners were accepted as citizens. The largest group? Twenty thousand ethnic Chinese.

Doing business with other races was normal, but racially mixing through marriage was still unusual and frowned upon, even by many young people. Some explained it as the result of centuries of attempted domination by the Chinese and Japanese, fueling a determination to remain a separate people. Whatever the reason, it was in sharp contrast to the civic religion of diversity that many Americans believed was required. Who was right? she asked herself.

Okay," she said, "I'll meet you at Namdaemun."

Originally, she had planned to wander around downtown Seoul, soaking up the sights and sounds after being away for almost a year. But she welcomed the chance to share stories with her old friend. In fact, she'd intended to call her while walking the streets under the tall, glowing neon signs; however, she'd expected that Sally would be absorbed in studying for one of her pre-med courses at north Seoul's Korea University.

She got off the train at the Myeondong station, north of the huge Namsan Park. Behind her the lower cable car station led up to the top of a hill and the north Seoul Tower, not unlike similar structures in Toronto and Kuala Lumpur, the main feature for visitors being a stunning 360° degree view of the city. The area was a grand place to tie on a pair of running shoes and hit the many trails through the park. As for tonight, she turned her attention to a market a few blocks west of the subway.

Maintaining a good walking pace, she slipped effortlessly between the groups and couples on the crowded sidewalk. As she neared the biggest open market in the country, literally hundreds of stalls selling everything from clothing to food, her inner guide—female intuition—caused her to stop and look back. A slight shadow disappearing into a doorway tipped her off. Ducking behind a hanging display of multi-colored kites, she waited several minutes. Then a casually-dressed young man appeared, glancing rapidly right and left. When the man raised a cell phone to his lips and spoke, not 30 seconds passed before another man joined him. For Lisa, that confirmed she was being followed.

After the men went off in different directions, she left the kite shop and went through the Namdaemun market to the food stalls. Sally waved to her in Korean fashion, arm outstretched, the palm down, moving only her fingers. Lisa walked faster and embraced her dearest friend. It would have been proper for both to bow to each other, but they were like twin sisters.

"How have you been?" Sally asked in English.

"Working hard, like you," Lisa replied.

"Your mother is well?"

"Very well. And your family?"

"They are enjoying good fortune," Sally said, and laughed. "What shall we eat tonight?"

"Choi's stall makes the best *bulgogi*, the marinated beef melts in your mouth."

"And Rhee's has the most delicious *galbi* in Seoul. I'd eat his barbecued short ribs everyday if I could afford it!"

Lisa shook her head. "Know what I missed most in America?"

"K-pop?" Sally teased, knowing her serious-minded friend preferred classical music, western or Korean.

"No, silly. I was dying for a hot bowl of beef noodle soup with prawn tempura, just like mother makes."

Sally assumed an air of solemnity. "Then that is what you shall have, young scholar."

Lisa put a hand over her mouth, stifling a laugh, as Sally their orders for the Korean soup. Finding an open table was not easy. But they persisted and eventually settled down with steaming bowls. It was just like old times, the year apart notwithstanding. Of course, they had called, texted and e-mailed during the interval, but heavy class loads and late nights studying took priority. Even weekends were crammed with time at their college's respective libraries. Finally, the meal consumed, both girls contented themselves with small talk. As the evening turned to night, Lisa leaned closer to her friend.

"I might need your help. Can I count on you?"

Sally, her pleasing Chinese features—jet black hair in a ponytail, mascara at the eyes, a touch of red lipstick above a delicate chin, and a short-sleeve print dress that fell to her knees, revealing shapely legs—were overcome by a look of unabashed curiosity. "You know I will help in any way I can. What is it, Jin Sun?"

The use of her Korean name told the story. Lisa knew she could depend on her friend, no matter what. As a matter of fact, she had known the answer before asking. It was just a way to broach a subject that had been on her mind since the afternoon encounter with a man going by the name of Roh.

"I was approached today with a story about how my father died. Not the official version...it was quite different. I think the same man is going to contact me again."

"Who is he and what did he want?"

"I'm certain he is attached to our security services."

"What does he want from you?" Sally asked again.

The noise of pots and pans banging, dishes being filled, people talking, chairs scraping—there was no way anyone could overhear them in the busy night market.

"He mentioned something about looking for a volunteer."

Sally sipped cold tea. "Volunteer for what?"

"I don't know."

"Have you told your mother?"

"He said not to, but I told her a few things." Lisa placed the chopsticks on top of the bowl, fiddled with them. "If anything happens..."

"Like what, Jin Sun? We are in the middle of the largest city in modern South Korea. We are not at war."

"Not yet."

"What does that mean? The North Koreans are acting up as usual and the Americans are unhappy about it. Life goes on. It always has."

Lisa nodded. "It has...since 1953."

"Okay, there was a war. It's over. Everyone has too much to lose by another conflict. Don't they?"

Lisa sighed. "You will help me?"

Sally nodded emphatically. "Cross my heart and hope to die."

They were interrupted by a shout from a few tables away. "There she is!"

As Lisa followed the voice, she recognized the speaker, the same guy as by the kite stall. By then he was only a few feet from their table and Lisa stood up, grabbed her friend's unfinished glass of tea and flung it in the man's face and kicked the side of his left knee. As he lost balance and banged into an empty chair and table, Lisa took Sally's arms and helped her up, then held onto her right wrist and pulled her away from the dining area. The place had grown unusually quiet. Everyone stared at them as they dashed from the market. In the darkness of an alley Lisa paused long enough for Sally to catch her breath.

"What was that all about?" Sally gasped.

"He followed me here."

"Why would he do that?"

"If I had an answer, I'd tell you," Lisa said impatiently. "Look, I'm sorry. One of my martial arts teachers advised, 'When in doubt, strike out.' So that's what I did. Teacher wasn't leading a class in Aikido."

Her friend stepped out into the main road and hailed a taxi. "I'm taking you back to your place. Don't argue, Jin Sun."

"Well, I *am* kind of on edge," she conceded.

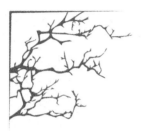

Chapter 8

AT HER APARTMENT LISA insisted on paying her share of the fare. Sally waved goodbye as the vehicle left for the short drive to her family's apartment in the nearby Gangnam district, also south of the Han River. Safely inside, Lisa tried to relax with a hot bath, then played with her dog. Heidi rolled onto her back, inviting a chest and belly rub, and that's precisely what her master gave her. Then she told her mother about the meal with Sally Chu, leaving out the incident at the market. Maybe it was just a case of mistaken identity, like in an old Alfred Hitchcock movie. Only that wasn't very comforting, considering the outcomes in some of those films.

Bringing the dog's crate into her bedroom, she left the plastic crate's metal door open and lay down on her bed. She put on a pair of tortoiseshell-framed reading glasses and opened a thick volume. The book was Alexander Solzhenitsyn's *Into the First Circle*, a novelistic account by the Nobel Prize-winning Russian author about political prisoners inside a scientific research center during the rule of the Soviet Union's dictator, Josef Stalin, in the 1950s.

Heavy reading for a young woman? she said to herself. Perhaps. But an attempt to understand what her fellow Koreans north of the demilitarized zone had to endure did not seem like a waste of time. After all, her father had given his life to hold the forces of evil at bay. She'd tried to read the usual popular teen books on vampires and zombies, the *Hunger Games* and *Game of Thrones* type of fantasies, often with a girl surviving chaos and becoming of a heroine. Americans loved heroes, she decided.

No doubt, some stories were well-written, but they seemed like commercially-motivated potboilers, designed to draw money from teens and young adults, a form of luxury entertainment to be indulged in while living in a relatively safe country. Compared to the reality of life in Seoul, with over one million soldiers of the Korean People's Army committed to destroying the democratic nation of South Korea, the publishers and authors in America could afford to mine the spending habits of students and young workers and get rich off their readers. Contrast that to the socialist society north of the DMZ, where 25 million led lives in unquestioning obedience and loyalty to a young North Korean leader who encouraged the same soul-deadening Cult of Personality as Stalin had so many years ago.

The thought of such monstrous dictators, past and present, reminded her of another Solzhenitsyn book, a slim paperback, also on her shelf. *One Day in the Life of Ivan Denisovich* had, surprisingly, been published in the early 1960s in the Soviet Union during what was considered a cultural thaw allowed by the head of the Communist Party to demonstrate a break from the tightly-controlled society during the Stalinist regime. That tale of a political prisoner banished to a labor camp in Siberia, a typical day of striving to survive the bitter cold, hard manual labor and near-starvation diet, led her mind back to the situation in North Korea.

The founder of that Communist country, Kim Il-Sung, had been chosen to rule the northern part of the Korean peninsula after WWII. The Soviets controlled the territory and selected Kim to lead the new nation in 1948, a choice seconded by Communist China's leader Mao Tse-tung. As Kim adopted many of the policies and traits of Josef Stalin, life in the north became a copycat country, a land of political oppression, a one-party state where the Communist Party was the sole determinant of right and wrong...all funneled through the person of Kim Il-Sung as Supreme Leader. Citizens learned to submit to the state's propaganda and control or they disappeared.

In California, Lisa had seen a map of North Korean concentration camps, published in a local newspaper. It was estimated that up to two hundred thousand men, women and children were confined in the camps, forced to labor on what soldiers called "short rations." To say that the North Korean population was brainwashed by the government's constant bombardment of propaganda, extolling the Kim family regime, was an understatement. Although fully a quarter of its national income went to the military, a substantial amount was spent annually on the various security services and units of the Thought Control police. Every North Korean was watched. Watched in school, watched at work, watched at play. Informers were everywhere, even in one's own family, a situation not unlike which prevailed in East Germany during the years of the Cold War in Europe.

Like most South Koreans, Lisa knew the troubled history of her country. Still, it was the daily challenges that occupied most people, as everywhere else on earth. The intense pressure on young people to do well in school and score high marks on the college entrance examination followed an ancient tradition in East Asia, dating back centuries when students in China went to the capital to take the examinations to become a Mandarin, a learned scholar. Also, in South Korea, young men were required to perform at least two years military service during their 20s. While the south had experienced remarkable economic growth for many years, its democratic practices had taken a bumpy path to the present. Corruption at the highest levels of government was a constant problem.

Finally, Lisa shelved her novel. She did not feel depressed or hopeless. Rather, she possessed a positive vision of the future, in spite of the challenges ahead. Perhaps her generation would find a way to live in peace with her fellow Koreans north of the DMZ. She decided that such a prospect was worth some kind of sacrifice. Then she laughed softly at her "noble" vision. Reaching up, she clicked off the light, pulled a wool blanket over and soon fell asleep.

The phone vibrating under her pillow woke her up. "Yes," she answered sleepily.

"Sorry," the man's voice said. "I woke you up?"

"Mr. Roh? Why are you calling now, sir?"

"Tomorrow morning you are free?"

"Yes."

"Meet me at the Jeoldusan Martyr's Shrine at nine o'clock. Goodnight."

Just like that, her itinerary for the morrow was set. She turned off her phone. No more late night interruptions.

It was the end of a very unusual day in Seoul.

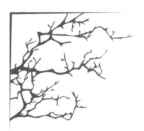

Chapter 9

BESIDE THE CHAPEL, Roh stood like a statue in a dark blue suit, a black umbrella shielding his uncovered head from the drizzle. He did not turn at the sound of footsteps on the flagstones.

"You want to know why I asked to see you here, Jin Sun?"

As he turned his head to look at his visitor, Lisa bowed her head, a sign of respect to an elder, then opened her own umbrella, a white one emblazoned with a design of the Rose of Sharon, the country's favorite flower. The red hibiscus blossom on the umbrella brightened an otherwise dreary morning. Roh bent down, took a metal flask, opened it and, after pouring steaming coffee into a plastic cup, offered it to his guest. With a shake of her head, Lisa declined and looked over the cliff at the gray waters of the Han River.

"I am not a Catholic," Roh confided, also gazing at the river. The steady drone of traffic on the riverside freeway reached up to them on the hill. It was not a place for quiet contemplation. "However, I cannot forget what was done on this ground in 1866. You know the story. Everyone in Seoul does."

"People choose not to think about it. It was just an unfortunate part of history," she countered.

"There are more Christians in our country today than there are Buddhists. It was not always so. Many foreigners find that surprising for an Asian land."

Lisa shrugged. "Half of our people don't associate with any belief system."

"Freethinkers. And yet, amazingly, our citizens manage to support sixty thousand fortune-tellers. What does it all mean?"

"It means, in education, what college will I be able to attend? In business, what company will I work for? In love, who will I marry? Those are the questions people want answered. For money, the fortune-tellers give them what they seek."

Suddenly, Roh smiled. "You have wisdom beyond your years, Jin Sun. That is one reason I am depending on you."

"Depend on me? For what, Mr. Roh?"

The official sipped his coffee, taking time to frame his words. "You are a follower of the one known as Jesus of Nazareth?"

"I believe that the Bible tells us the historical truth about Jesus' life, death and resurrection. I believe He is God the Son."

"A difficult concept, God the Father, God the Son, God the Holy Spirit. One God in three persons. Who can understand it?"

"Isn't it arrogant to expect that a human mind can perfectly understand our Creator?"

Now Roh shook his head, still grinning. "Your father and mother have taught you well."

"Father told me that he had no spiritual beliefs when he joined the army. Later, his conscience woke up, as he put it. He had a friend who left the military after becoming a member of the Society of Friends, a group of Christians known as Quakers."

"Pacifists."

"Exactly. Father attended services with his friend, even joined the church. When he questioned the practice of making war on other countries, an officer and senior NCO listened carefully to him and, in the end, convinced him that it was not possible to live one's life consistent with pacifism, not in this world. 'Blessed are the Peacemakers,' Jesus said, but even the Bible is full of war and struggle. Father re-enlisted. He referred to himself as 'the only Fighting Quaker.' You know the rest."

"The day he died I recalled one of the few Bible verses I am acquainted with. Your Lord Jesus said, 'Those who live by the sword shall die by the sword.' Then again, we shall all die one day, every one of us."

She gestured downward. "1866, on this spot, 2,000 Koreans, members of the Roman Catholic Church, were slain. Many were beheaded, their bodies thrown off this cliff to the river below as part of a mass execution. This is now Holy Ground, purchased with the blood of martyrs."

"So you believe those Christians did not die in vain?"

"I'd like to believe that my dad did not lose his life for nothing," she answered quietly.

Roh was silent.

Lisa collapsed her umbrella, shook it. The rain had stopped, though a cool wind was sweeping down from the hills in the northwest, driving away the usual smells of the large city—diesel exhaust, smoke from coal-burning plants and factories, the odors of millions of people. As for Roh's silence, it seemed to portend his satisfaction with her reply.

"Mr. Roh, you did not request my presence here to discuss history," she prompted.

"Eh? Oh, excuse me. As a matter of fact, history is precisely why we are here." He screwed the plastic cup onto the flask, set it on the ground. "You are obviously well-read. Does the name Dietrich Bonhoeffer mean anything to you?"

"Last year, I read his '*Letters and Papers from Prison.*'"

Roh let out a low whistle of appreciation. "Like I said, I am not a believer. However, I have great admiration for people of courage. Bonhoeffer, as you know, was a Lutheran pastor in Germany during the rise of Adolf Hitler to power. He became a leader of the Confessional Church, the sole Christian organization in wartime Germany that protested the oppressive and discriminatory policies of the Nazi Party. For his outspoken preaching on the regime's excesses, Bonhoeffer was closely watched by the Gestapo, the state's secret police. The debate within the Confessional Church and with some officers in the German Army—the Wehrmacht—concerned the need to remove Hitler from power before the madman destroyed all of Germany. As a result, Bonhoeffer reached the bold conclusion that it was better for one man to die than that a whole nation should go down in flames. His part in a failed plot to blow up Hitler was discovered and he was imprisoned. Days before the allies reached Flossenburg, the prison where he and others were held, Pastor Bonhoeffer was hanged."

Roh set his open umbrella on the grass. A gust of wind caught the fabric and sent it sailing out over the cliff. Roh watched it float onto the river. "Lisa, I have a proposition for you."

"I hope you're not expecting me to sneak into North Korea and assassinate Kim Jong-Un," she said, and laughed at the absurdity of her own statement.

The bells of the chapel rang out, startling both of them. As the bells continued to ring, men and women walked into the church. When it was quiet again, Roh turned to face his young companion, the look on his face deadly serious.

"I have been ordered to send someone into the north to avenge Warrant Officer Park's death. We have now identified the home of Pak Chul in Pyongyang."

"Didn't you say it was Pak Chul's son, Captain Pak Sung that shot down my father's helicopter?"

"I also explained that targeting an army officer in the field is extremely difficult."

"My dad was singled out and he was on duty by the DMZ."

Roh nodded. "Your logic is sound. Nevertheless, my superiors prefer to strike at an old foe whose crime has gone unanswered far too long. The result will be a symbolic victory." Roh took her by the elbow, led her away from the cliff to the car park and a waiting black Kia sedan. "If you will allow me a few more hours, I would like you to accompany me on a short drive out of the city."

Lisa, bitten by the curiosity bug, climbed into the back seat of the car and sat behind a driver dressed in civilian clothes.

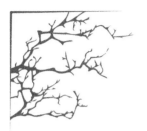

Chapter 10

BLACK CLOUDS HAD ASSEMBLED over the rocky and tree-strewn slopes northwest of the capital and thunder rumbled ominously, an occasional loud crack breaking through the noise of traffic on the drive out of the Seoul metropolitan area. Roh's driver piloted the car skillfully through the stream of trucks, vans and cars until they were clear of the city. Now and then, Lisa spotted a jagged line of light cutting down from the heavens to the earth, lightning that erupted for a second, then quickly disappeared. Heading northward, rain began to pelt the vehicle, the drops coming down sporadically at first before changing to the large, heavy drops of a downpour. Even the wipers on fast speed were not enough to completely clear the windshield. The driver switched the ventilation system on high to clear moisture off the windows and, in the fast lane, ploughed through the spray kicked up by articulated trucks.

The amount of truck traffic going north empty and heading south fully-loaded toward Seoul or the Port of Incheon puzzled her, since the no man's land of the DMZ lay directly ahead. "What does so much civilian traffic to and from the demilitarized zone mean, Mr. Roh?"

"No doubt you have noticed the increasingly industrialized and populous northern districts of Seoul," he began. "Well, the main source of the trucks and the car carriers is the Kaesong Industrial Complex, located just inside North Korea. Due to our shortage of labor and determination not to rely on immigrants, our government fashioned an agreement with Kim's regime. Led by Hyundai, more than a hundred South Korean businesses operate in a special sector of the Democratic People's Republic of Korea. Over fifty thousand North Koreans work in manufacturing plants, turning out auto parts, clothing, and kitchen items. Economically it is good for our country and, for the north, a source of much-needed currency."

"Who is in charge of these operations?"

"South Korean managers pass through a checkpoint in the DMZ daily. Of course, there are plenty of Kim's security agents in the complex, spying on their own people, especially to prevent unwanted contact between their workers and those from our country. Their security people thoroughly screen North Koreans before allowing them to work there, as well as keeping an eye out for any sign of a potential defector. Transportation vehicles, commercial and private, are searched before leaving the complex. Industrial espionage is a concern for our businesses, too."

"It seems an odd arrangement."

"Some in our government hope that it will discourage North Korea from trying to destroy our country. Regarding international trade, they are almost totally dependent on China and on us." Roh used his coat sleeve to clear a fogged window. "Hard to believe, but true."

She wanted to ask him where they were going but sensed it was better to hold her questions, as if she was being evaluated...and the ability to hold one's tongue was an important factor in the process.

Eventually the car pulled up at a hilly area that had been cleared of trees, with the fence and watchtowers of the DMZ visible. She looked for the one-story blue- painted huts and the stark, two-story ceremonial building at Panmunjom, site of the armistice talks to end the Korean conflict; instead, she found green rolling hills and, inside the DMZ, a plowed center, vacant of human activity. Roh opened his door, got out with a black umbrella and waited for her to join him.

"Do you want to know why I brought you here?"

She waited for his explanation.

"Not fifty yards from where we stand, your father's helicopter crash-landed. His aircraft had been flying south of the DMZ, not inside it as the North Koreans claimed."

Lisa looked west to the spot Roh indicated. She did not move.

"The demilitarized zone runs across the land for 152 miles, connecting the Yellow Sea in the west with the East Sea, or Sea of Japan, on the east coast. Two and a half miles wide, it forms the northern boundary of our country, a man-made barrier between us and 25 million Koreans in the north." While shielding her with his umbrella, Roh took out a pack of cigarettes and lit one. "You don't smoke? That is good. For me, it is a crutch familiar to policemen around the world. On long stakeouts and static surveillance, the nicotine helps keep the mind alert; otherwise, a filthy habit."

"I understand Mr. Roh. Go on, please." Glancing again to the land of her father's last breath, she straightened her shoulders. "I am prepared to listen to everything you have to say."

Roh raised his left arm to the north. "On the other side of the DMZ lies an army of over one million, ready to go to war at a moment's notice. Only the United States, China and India maintain a larger military. The North Koreans also have a reserve force of about seven million; in effect, one third of their population is either on active duty with the military or on standby status. From birth, their soldiers have been indoctrinated by the regime's propaganda that America was the aggressor in the Korean War and still seeks to destroy their country. That military machine gobbles up over a quarter of North Korea's modest total income, year after year." He took a long draw on his cigarette, exhaled through his nostrils. "The firepower aimed at our forces and largest city, Seoul, is immense. While the historical center of the DMZ at Panmunjom is where tourists visit, this sector is where the greatest threat is concentrated." He took a pair of Asahi Pentax 7x35 binoculars from the car's front seat and passed them to her. "Take a look for yourself."

As she adjusted the black binoculars, focusing the lenses more clearly, the rain let up, replaced by low, scudding clouds that partially-obscured the landscape. Other than the sounds of trucks on the nearby expressway, the place was eerily quiet. No helicopters operated in the low ceiling conditions—no Black Hawks, Apache gunships or Chinook troop carriers. The sounds of massive armies facing off was absent on this late morning in June. Then she saw them, long tubes protruding over brush and scrub, partly hidden by trees, poplars mostly. Standing under the cover of a roofed wooden observation tower, a North Korean soldier peered back at her with field glasses. She wondered if the observer was none other than Pak Sung, the man who had ordered her father's Black Hawk shot down. By his shoulder boards she knew he was an officer, but could not discern the rank.

"I assume we have artillery batteries facing down our enemy?" She traded the binoculars for his umbrella.

"Enough to make it a standoff. We call ours 'counter-battery units,' designed to respond immediately to any aggression." He placed the Japanese-made binoculars back in their leather case, hung the strap from his shoulder. Field-stripping his cigarette, he pocketed the tar-stained filter. "We are looking at units of North Korea's Second Corps. We estimate they possess 500 pieces of artillery, a significant number even though some date back many decades. It is difficult to accurately assess the status of their ammunition stockpiles, but we believe their forces on the DMZ are not merely showpieces. They are not bluffing. In addition," he lit another cigarette with his battered Zippo lighter, "there are large formations of North Korean forces on either side of this one near Kaesong. In short, the potential damage to the people and facilities of Seoul is enormous. Imagine, Jin Sun, half of our nation's population—25 million people—live and work within the range of the north's artillery!"

Lowering the umbrella, she said, "After the Korean War, why didn't our leaders establish a new capital in, say, Busan, far to the south?"

"Historically, Seoul has been our capital, going back over 500 years. It is the place of our royal palaces. Frankly, until twenty-five years after the Korean War, the reality of field artillery accurately firing projectiles at targets over 20 miles away was not considered. As ranges have extended and accuracy has improved...well, it it too late." He shrugged. "The reality today is that the north can shell the Seoul area with up to forty thousand rounds an hour. A recent study places the casualties, mostly civilian, at over 64,000 dead within hours. They also possess 2 or 3 dozen multiple rocket launchers, massive 300mm guns that can shoot eight rockets every quarter hour, with an effective range of over 40 miles. That's far enough to reach beyond central Seoul to the southern suburbs. But instead of emphasizing industrial growth southward, beyond the range of our enemy's guns, the government has bowed to business demands to open up land north of the capital for industry. In other words, *closer* to the DMZ."

"So our leaders do not seriously believe that a conflict is inevitable," she added.

"It may not be up to us as South Koreans, Jin Sun."

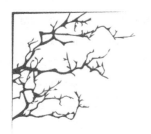

Chapter 11

A SOUND LIKE GUNFIRE erupted and, involuntarily, Lisa jumped. She saw an old army jeep approaching, backfiring again. As it rolled to a halt a young officer wearing green-and-brown camouflage fatigues and helmet climbed down. The Korean officer strolled up to them, a hard look on his unlined face as he unsnapped the flap of his holster. Roh's driver got out of the car, one hand sliding inside his jacket. Roh shook his head, let the cigarette hang from his mouth and produced a leather ID wallet. He snapped it open and the Korean soldier saluted, then gestured to his own driver and a rifle-carrying enlisted man on the back seat.

"Sorry, sir," the officer said, "you were spotted in this restricted area. I was sent to clarify your status."

Once again, Roh calmly tore up the unburned paper of his cigarette, let it fall to the ground and kept the filter. "At ease, lieutenant. The purpose of our visit is on a—"

"Need to know basis," the officer finished.

"Lieutenant, I was explaining official matters to this young lady. A visual confirmation of my words is invaluable."

The officer looked to the north. "You know that you are being watched?"

"Part of the training," Roh responded.

Lisa thought the officer looked very handsome. "May we know your name?" she said.

The officer allowed a half-smile. "Myung. I am Lieutenant Myung."

Roh said, "As part of her education, would you mind elaborating on the north's missile capabilities?"

"That's not my area of responsibility, sir."

"Surely, you are well-informed on the subject."

"Well, sir," Myung began, "their Hwasong-7 missile has a range of up to 600 miles. The No-Dong 1 can fly over 900 miles. The former threatens our entire country, plus Japan. The latter is, possibly, capable of reaching the northern part of Taiwan. We assume that Beijing would not be targeted."

"What about nuclear warheads?"

The officer hooked his thumbs in the webbing-belt that held his gear. "Again, not my specialty, sir. I suspect that you possess the most recent information on that subject."

"Pretend that I know nothing. What can you tell us?"

"What I am aware of suggests that Kim Jong-Un's forces have developed their satellite launch vehicle, the Taepodong-2 into an ICBM with an expected range in excess of nine thousand miles. Quite possibly they now possess the capability of reaching cities in the United States."

"What do you think of the meeting between North Korea's 'Supreme Leader' and the American president?"

"Don't ask me about politics, sir. My job is to be prepared for the worst."

"Thank you, lieutenant. Your cooperation will be noted." Roh signaled to his driver to prepare to leave. "Oh, one more thing."

"Sir?"

"Can you imagine a scenario where the north launches a full-out attack on our country?"

"That is why I continue to wear the uniform."

"Ah, so they would dare destroy the 'goose that lays the golden egg?' We represent a significant part of their foreign trade. They need us, don't they?"

"Sir, you already know the answer to that question."

Roh smiled. "Please, I'd really like to know what you think."

"The people of North Korea, their huge military and security establishment, exist to preserve and protect the leaders in Pyongyang. From military history, I'd say that Kim Jong-Un is a likely candidate to follow the example of Adolf Hitler and bring down his entire country in a losing war, rather than surrender the power and wealth he enjoys."

"So you don't believe he will surrender his nuclear arsenal."

"Do you, sir?"

Roh bowed his head slightly to the younger man...an unusual mark of respect.

The officer saluted again and returned to his jeep.

As the army patrol drove away, Lisa asked, "Such an old vehicle. Whatever happened to the Hummers?"

"Humvees. The military version is known as a Humvee. Anyway, the Jeep is like an old trusted weapon, something worth keeping." He guided her away from the car. "Now I have to ask you an important question, Park Jin Sun."

"I am ready, Mr. Roh."

"You have seen the place your father gave his life for our people. You have witnessed part of the threat facing half of our country's population. You have seen the determination of our troops and how they are prepared to risk their lives for our freedom."

She nodded.

Taking out his Zippo lighter, Roh opened and snapped it shut, over and over. "Did you know that this was a gift from your father, Warrant Officer Park?"

She shook her head. "He never told me."

"He got it at his army's post exchange a month before..."

"Father spoke little of his military duties. I think he wanted to protect us from the ugly reality."

Finally, the decision made, Roh returned the lighter to his coat pocket. "Lisa, we need to insert someone into Pyongyang. We want Pak Chul eliminated."

"The father of my dad's killer," she said softly.

"It is a dangerous mission. I cannot promise success or even a safe return."

"You are asking me to do this?"

Roh studied the little bubbles of water that had collected on his polished black shoes. Looking up he said, "As a friend of your father's, I would advise you to turn down the assignment. I cannot over-emphasize the hazards an agent will face in that paranoid and unforgiving land."

"Then you will send someone else," she said.

"That is certain."

She took a deep breath. "I will do this thing. For my father and for my country."

"You cannot tell your mother where you are going."

"She will be safe?"

Roh shrugged. "Is anyone here truly safe?"

"You know what I mean."

"Yes, we will protect her." Roh led her back to the car, opened the rear passenger door. "We know about your experience at the Namdaemun market."

"Men were following me."

"You witnessed the assassination on the subway. The victim, a high-ranking defector from Pyongyang, was talking to us. His killer did not act alone. There were watchers in the vicinity, to confirm the man's death and to verify that the assassin made good his getaway." Roh rubbed his chin. "Most likely, you were spotted near the motorcycle used in the escape, and then, speaking to a policeman."

"They know where I live?"

"I don't think so. But they will, given enough time." Roh smiled. "You handled yourself exceptionally well, Jin Sun. As you did earlier in the park with the purse-snatcher."

"So your people have been watching me, too?"

"The nature of the game we play. It is very serious. As now you know."

"My mother?"

"Will be moved to a safe house, somewhere in eastern Seoul. I'm afraid she will have to take a leave of absence from work. Even after you return, she may not be able to resume her current business. It will require new identities for both of you."

"Thank you for that vote of confidence."

"Oh?"

"That I might return."

"Yes, of course." He coughed. "And she will not be alone, Jin Sun."

"No?"

"She will have your dog for company."

A lighter moment in the preparations, Lisa realized. "In the north, I will operate alone?"

"Not entirely alone. I am not prepared to say more at this time."

"When do I leave?"

"Your plane leaves this evening."

"I thought that Kim's regime does not welcome South Koreans."

"That policy has loosened recently. In any case, your flight will land in Beijing."

"China?"

"North Korea's protector. Your cover story begins there."

"So all the years of studying Mandarin is going to pay off," she said, trying to sound confident.

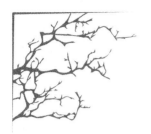

Chapter 12

THE AIR OVER THE CHINESE capital was hazy, the sky filled with yellow particles of sand and dust carried eastward from the deserts of Mongolia. As the China Eastern Airlines Boeing jetliner neared Beijing Capital International Airport, Lisa's thoughts went back to her journey to South Korea's ultra-modern Incheon International, west of Seoul. After Roh's driver had deposited a smooth aluminum carry-on case in the trunk of the Kia sedan, Lisa had sat in back with Mr. Roh. Her controller used the time to brief his newly-recruited agent.

"You are travelling light, Jin Sun. You will stay overnight in the Chinese capital and receive official travel documents, basic instruction on counter-surveillance techniques—no time for practical training—and intense indoctrination in your cover story. Tomorrow morning, you fly to Pyongyang with a small group of businesspeople, a trip organized in accordance with North Korea's practice of welcoming only hosted groups. Your group has been coordinated with an office dealing with foreign investment and cooperative ventures. You will only by in Pyongyang for two days, so you will have to work fast."

"You know where Pak Chul lives?"

"Memorize it." Roh unfolded a paper with the address of a large apartment building in central Pyongyang. He took out his pack of cigarettes. "Our best information is that he is semi-retired and in poor health. Probably suffers from COPD as a result of years of smoking." Roh fiddled with the unopened pack, then put away his cigarettes.

"There is a guard?"

"It is not military housing, mostly Party workers and government bureaucrats. If a concierge is on duty, a distraction will be arranged."

"By me?"

"Your contact, whom you will meet at the apartment. Enough said about that for now."

"What if Pak Chul is home, but refuses to let me in?"

"You are a student of history at Pyongyang University. He is a hero of the revolutionary struggle. You want to interview him on his famous role in the DPRK's struggle with the imperialists." Roh sat back in his seat. "Believe me, an old man of his stature cannot resist such interest from a young woman."

Lisa gazed at him skeptically.

"As last resort, announce that you have seen the fire brigade in the building, that there is smoke in the hallways on the floor below. Tell him that he should evacuate while the source of the smoke is investigated. He will open the door."

"Okay," she agreed, "that ought to work."

"I think the student writing-a-paper story fits best. Try to stick with it. If you must use the fire story, make it clear you are acting as a good citizen. Trust me on this."

"Shouldn't an appointment be set up by letter or telephone?"

"You are just a poor student, without regular access to a phone. Few North Koreans have cell phones. We can arrange for a general letter of introduction to be created, leaving out his name. Add that and your faculty's name before sliding the paper under his door." Roh sat up straight, looked her in the eye. "You are smart enough to improvise. The main thing is, you have the right motivation."

"Yes."

"Lose the emotional element now, Jin Sun," he said sharply. "Do you think you can do that?"

She broke eye contact and stared through the windshield at the modern airport. The sound of commercial aircraft taking off and landing intruded. "I...I'm not sure."

"An honest reply. Listen, you are an amateur, untested in the field. For this mission, you must tightly control your emotions. Steel yourself and focus entirely on the job." He checked his wristwatch. "Know that you will be watched from the moment you board that plane in Beijing tomorrow. The crew watch the passengers *and* each other. The regime keeps their families hostage, ensuring that pilots and flight attendants on international runs do not defect while out of the country. Just keep in mind that you will be under constant surveillance by State Security during your short stay in Pyongyang. Your group's guide is obligated to accompany you while outside your hotel. If a visitor leaves a group, the guide faces the likelihood of hard labor in a camp. Make no mistake, after you slip away, your guide will be severely punished. In this case, maybe even executed."

"That isn't fair!"

"I will not lie to you. Our government wants to send a strong message after yesterday's assassination on the subway."

"So it's not because of my father?"

"It is for me."

"I don't understand."

"Nor do *I* understand all things. I am following orders from high up in the National Intelligence Service. What I can tell you is that, ever since your father's helicopter was downed—and I joined the agency soon afterward—a great deal of planning has gone into a retaliatory strike as punishment for their unjustified action." The sedan slowed and entered a departure lane. Roh smoothed his hair, adjusted his tie knot. "From the beginning, I considered you for the act of vengeance over your father's death. I spoke to no one about it. It would have been considered unprofessional."

She nodded slowly, studied her hands.

"It is not too late to back out, Jin Sun. No one will blame you."

She sighed. "I will do this to honor my father."

"A good reason."

She brightened. "Besides, I am on school break and I'm not into K-pop. Instead, I get to enjoy international travel, learn new customs, see for myself what life is like north of the 38th Parallel."

"That's the spirit," Roh encouraged. The car drew level with a sign posted at the terminal for China Eastern Airlines. The driver got out, opened the trunk and took out her carry-on luggage, while Roh handed her the airline ticket, a wad of Chinese currency—yuan in notes of several denominations—and her passport. "An associate got the document from your apartment while advising your mother that you are traveling to China on government business."

"How did she take the news?"

"She is worried...not knowing any details. But she is a strong woman. It was explained that the move to the safe house is just a routine precaution." He got out, waited for her to join him outside the terminal. "You will be met on arrival by one of ours. Listen carefully to her this evening and tomorrow morning. She has much to teach you in a short period of time. It will seem like cramming for an exam, which you are very good at. Also, she will supply the weapons—ordinary items that won't arouse suspicion—and demonstrate how they work."

"How will I recognize her?"

"Like looking in a mirror," Roh said cryptically.

The flight went smoothly but she was relieved when the landing gear lowered and the plane landed at the modern Beijing airport. She brought down her bag and walked through the busy terminal to the stylish departure building which she likened to a massive, artfully-designed Quonset hut. Then again, she reminded herself, she was not a student of art history or architecture. She was on a secret assignment, tasked with ending the life of a cruel man who, by rights, should've already been executed or, at the very least, imprisoned for his criminal actions. There was no honor in what the man had done in uniform decades ago, an example followed, tragically—perhaps inevitably—by his son. In her mind, there was the image of a white stone cross in a cemetery filled with lines of tombstones.

"An eye for an eye," she whispered to herself. "Sometimes we can't just turn the other cheek. Forgive me, Lord."

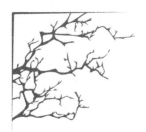

Chapter 13

PAUSING AT THE END of the departure hall, she saw a vision of herself bathed in the natural light pouring down from the hall's curved overhead windows. After blinking her eyes, she stared incredulously at the image of an identical twin. Same height, same weight, same facial features, except for the Chinese almond eyes, and those brown eyes were opened wide, sharing Lisa's astonishment. She set down her bag, covered her face with both hands and peeked through her spread fingers. Still there, her body double, just like in a Korean movie.

Her counterpart came up close, took her bag. "I am Khoo Huei Fun. And you are Park Jin Sun." With her free hand, the young Chinese woman shook Lisa's hand lightly. "I knew that somewhere in this world, I had a sister. Please, follow me. We will take the light-rail into the city."

"Yes, thank you," was all Lisa could manage, and walked alongside her contact.

"You will stay at my place, a small apartment in a boutique hotel not far from the Forbidden City complex. We have much to discuss, but it must wait until we are behind a locked door." Her guide took the aluminum carry-on and led the way to a ladies' restroom. "Take the stall next to mine," she said quietly, in Korean. "We will exchange clothes."

Not understanding the reason, Lisa complied with the direction, as Roh had instructed. Huei Fun could not restrain a giggle as she passed her skirt to Lisa. When they were finished changing, they left the bathroom. Back in the departure hall, Lisa, once again, was amazed at the appearance of the young woman standing opposite...a strikingly accurate look-alike, except for the shoes. Lisa wore her own, being a full size larger. Huei Fun reached into a fabric bag, took out a floppy red hat and a pair of sunglasses and put them on.

There had been no complications in the customs and immigration experience and Lisa tried to absorb the sights on the quick ride into Beijing. She recognized the Olympic facilities from seeing the games on television, then they were into the congested city. The air was thick with yellow dust and industrial and vehicular smog. Many citizens wore surgical masks as a protection from the particulates, not unlike in Seoul, which sometimes suffered from the free but unwanted Chinese export of polluted air. The monsoon rains did not easily reach as far inland as the capital of China and the sands blown in from Mongolia hit Beijing more directly than South Korea, four hundred miles to the east.

Getting down from the light-rail train, they switched to the Metro for the final run into the city center. From the subway station, it was a short walk to the apartment, located on Shajing Hutong, a busy lane just east of the Black Lakes, a mile north of the Forbidden City. Walking into the Bamboo Forest Hotel, a small facility of 50 rooms with a central courtyard decorated with hanging red lanterns, the staff bowed and greeted Lisa with many friendly words, addressing her as "Miss Khoo."

Lisa played along, using her excellent Mandarin to introduce her companion in the red hat and dark glasses as a business associate, "Lucy Kwan."

Safely in her apartment, Huei Fun took off the glasses and hat and collapsed on a bamboo chair, laughing at the deceit. "There is not much to enjoy in this business. That was fun." She reached back and switched on a portable CD player. The sounds of light jazz filled the small apartment—a one-bedroom affair with a kitchenette off the front room. "If you wish to wash up, the bathroom is next to the bedroom door. I'll make a pot of tea."

Lisa rinsed her hands and face, used the toilet and washed again, the grime of travel sent down the drain. Back in the living area, she not-

ed the scroll painting on the wall, a black horse rising up. There was also a vase of fresh-cut flowers, red hibiscus, in a painted vase on a small
table by the two-person sofa. The sofa and a small table for dining and
three hard chairs were all the furnishings, along with two lamps, one of
them freestanding. "The painting of the horse...it is yours?"

Her hostess nodded. "A touch of home. I always take it with me."

"Oh, so you are not staying here long?"

"After you have gone, I will roll it up, pack it with clothes in my
suitcase and check out."

"Where will you go?" Then Lisa held up a hand. "Sorry, maybe I
should not know that."

Huei Fun shook her head. "For everyone's benefit, it is best not to
know. But just between us girls, it will be somewhere in Asia." Once
more, she giggled. "I am 24 years old and you are nineteen. Have you a
boyfriend?"

Girl talk, conducted in English. "No time," Lisa said.

"Me neither. Anyway, our generation is getting married later. I must
establish myself in this profession first."

"You have gone on missions before?"

Huei Fun shook her head. "I am what you might call a junior case
officer, working under Mr. Roh."

"That really is his name?"

Huei Fun laughed. "Ask him next time you see him." She poured
tea into two cups, carried them to the small dining table. "Please, sit
down. We have a lot of material to go over and it is already nine
o'clock."

"I am used to staying up late."

Taking a pile of papers from next to the table, Huei Fun laid a typed
letter in front of Lisa. "Your generalized letter of introduction to the
target. In the morning you will collect your passport—actually *my* passport—and a visa to enter North Korea. A travel agency here in Beijing is handling the arrangements for the group you are traveling with,

a necessity with Kim's regime. Each visiting group must have a sponsoring organization in North Korea. You will fly on Koryo Airlines, the North's official international carrier. At the Pyongyang airport, you will be met by an official guide." She paused to sip tea. "He will be responsible for you and your group. Outside of your hotel, you must travel only in his company. If you wish to visit a site in Pyongyang, it must be with your guide."

"When I leave the group to accomplish my mission, what happens to the guide?"

"After your absence is discovered, an alert will go out with your physical description. The police will search for you. The guide will be in big trouble."

"Arrested?"

"And interrogated...not gently. Your escape will condemn him. It can't be helped, Lisa. It is *their* system." She then passed over a professionally-printed color brochure of several pages, photographs and general descriptions of auto parts handled by her company—rubber weather stripping, serpentine belts, floor mats, mud flaps. There was also a price list, noting typical wholesale prices. "Study these on the plane. There are duplicates in a folder you will carry in a lightweight briefcase to present to an official the day after tomorrow. The first day will consist of settling into your hotel, a welcoming dinner by representatives of your sponsor, a bit of time for sightseeing, organized and led by your guide, of course."

"Mostly rubber products," Lisa noted, paging through the brochure. "What do I know of rubber and auto parts?"

"Rubber bounces," her case officer teased. "It comes from rubber trees or is made from petroleum products, a synthetic variety. Look, my friend, you are not there as an expert. You are basically a saleswoman, presenting commercial opportunities for them to earn precious foreign currency by joining with us in erecting a manufacturing plant in North Korea. Although my parents live in Seoul, I am still Chinese, a citizen

of the People's Republic, and we are North Korea's biggest trading partner. They need our currency. We need their cheap labor. That is our
China-based company's official reason for offering a mutually-satisfac-
tory deal with Pyongyang."

"This company really exists?"

"Oh, yes. Real people, real manufacturing facilities near Shanghai,
real products from a subsidiary of a South Korean corporation." She
grinned, turned up the volume of the music. "Having said that, it is es-
sentially a well-disguised front organization for South Korea's intelligence agency. Now you know."

Lisa drank her tea, pushed aside the documents. "A question has
bothered me. I did not ask Mr. Roh for an answer."

"Try me."

"You know the identity of my target?"

Her case officer nodded. "Speak freely. This room is swept daily for
'bugs.' And the music muffles our voices."

"Do we know for certain that Pak Chul is alive?"

"A fair question."

"I mean, maybe he was punished years ago for bringing unwanted
attention to the regime of the Supreme Leader, Kim Il-Sung. Or perhaps Pak Chul died of natural causes?"

"The axe-murder incident Pak Chul is famous for could not, in
North Korea's centralized, militaristic society, have been his own impulsive idea. He was, undoubtedly, ordered to confront the American
work detail in the DMZ and force them, at great loss of face, to with-
draw. The arrival of reinforcements armed with metal pipes and axe
handles, implements used to inflict blunt object wounds, was not acci-
dental nor the result of one captain's order. Beating two U.S. Army officers to death was a provocative act called for and approved at the highest levels of the North Korean government, which has been tightly-controlled by the Kim family since the end of WWII." Huei Fun carefully
studied her young charge's reaction. "As for Pak Chul, we are reason-

ably sure he remains alive, though in failing health. Of course, because of his status as a hero of the army, one who fought valiantly for Kim Il-Sung's honor in direct conflict with the Americans, it is not unthinkable that the regime might want to extend his stay on earth. Even if that means an imposter now pretends to be the former Captain Pak Chul."

"The Supreme Leader's son, Kim Jong-Il, took a special interest in filmmaking, didn't he?"

"Yes. He was responsible for the abduction of South Korea's finest director and movie star wife. Four years passed while the two were separated, not knowing if the other lived. That director was compelled to make several movies for Kim Jong-Il before husband-and-wife managed to escape while on officially-approved film business in Europe. So the possibility exists that Pak Chul is dead, and yet continues to live in the person of a trained actor."

"Is all this effort worth it?"

"We think Pak Chul, the original monster, still occupies a place in this world. But even if he has passed into Hell, the death of his replacement will serve our purpose."

"Which is?"

The smile was wiped from Huei Fun's pretty face. "The same message they send by hunting down and killing defectors from their country...that we can get to anyone, anywhere. Even someone close to Kim Jong-Un."

Lisa was silent, the enormity of her undertaking sinking in.

"The survival of South Korea is everything." Huei Fun got up from her chair, went to the kitchenette. "Time to eat, then your training begins."

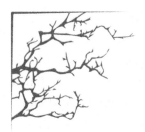

Chapter 14

A CLAUSTROPHOBIC SENSE of being trapped in an anonymous hotel room descended upon Lisa, a feeling that she fought against. She could have been in Singapore, Bangkok or Tokyo, such was her mood of disorientation. Reminders of where she was came from the noises outside the door, the nearly constant tramping of residents and guests in the hallway, loud talking and laughter coming up to the second floor from the courtyard, a toilet flushing in the room above, the abrasive hacking sound made in typical Chinese fashion before spitting, an obviously inebriated man loudly cursing someone in the room next door, even the sounds of cars and small delivery vans in the alley. The constant was that of spoken Mandarin. She was in China.

She helped her hostess fill small white bowls with rice, a plate with vegetables—bok choy, cucumber slices, bean sprouts—and a dish of boiled chicken. The simple meal, eaten with chopsticks, was accompanied by cups of strong black tea, partly offsetting the drowsy effects of food in the stomach. After eating, the young women shared clean-up duties.

By ten o'clock, they were back at the table, the freestanding lamp lighting a display of writing implements. Huei Fun explained, "Since your access to the target is predicated on the notion of conducting an interview, pens have been chosen as the most innocuous-looking weapons. For example," she picked up a silver-colored Cross pen and opened it, "this ink cartridge is labelled 'fine point.' In fact, our technicians have replaced the tip with a *very* fine point, one made of hardened steel that will pierce human flesh into the layer of subcutaneous fat or even muscle tissue." She brought the upper and lower halves of the pen back together and, taking a slip of blank paper, wrote circles and lines. "Even the ink has been reformulated to flow as from a regular fine point cartridge. Any questions?"

Lisa lifted the pen, examined it, wrote with it. "So it is used like an awl. I don't know much about tools, not like my father."

"My closest uncle is a master craftsman in leatherwork. He uses an awl to make holes."

"It is a killing object?"

"It can be."

"How am I expected to use this?"

Her case officer twisted the top half of the pen, retracting the point, and placed it at her throat. "Here, at the jugular vein. A forceful shove against an old man's neck will easily break through the thin skin and he will bleed profusely."

"How long must I wait for him to bleed to death? What if he struggles, calls for help?"

"First, you will disable him. I am told your Taekwondo is very good, so a hand strike to his neck, from behind or the front. If frontal, you will damage his trachea. A ruptured windpipe will lead to trouble breathing...he already has a lung problem. Choking for air, he will panic and not be able to call out. A strike at the back of the neck—as he cowardly did to the American major—will stun him, probably break a cervical bone. Then you pierce his vein. If you miss the vein and punch into the carotid artery, no problem. Except that he will spurt blood like a geyser."

"And I watch, hoping no one hears anything. What if he has a gun?"

"Not in North Korea. No privately-owned guns, even for their heroic army veteran. No," she lifted a Mount Blanc fountain pen, keeping her fingers off the pocket clip, "after you open a hole in a vein or artery, insert the tip of the fountain pen downward into his neck, press hard on the clip—which breaks open a capsule of poison—and the ink/poison mixture will drain into him. It doesn't take much to do the trick. I'm guessing that the capsule contains either sodium or potassium cyanide. It works very rapidly, Lisa. He will be dead in less than 15 seconds. Maybe one second only. Then you will clean off the pens and wipe down every surface you may have touched. Give yourself a couple of minutes, and listen carefully at the door before leaving." She placed the pen back on the table. "By the way, Pyongyang experiences shortages of both electricity *and* running water. Like most citizens, he will keep a bucket of water by the kitchen sink and in the bathroom. Because of sanitary problems in the north, you will carry a small bottle of unscented bleach to mix with water. Use the bleach to disinfect the pens of any human tissue samples and, first chance you get, toss them in a river or lake. Questions?"

"A million," Lisa said.

"How do you feel now?"

"Sick to my stomach," she admitted.

"That is only natural. When the moment comes, you will do fine. It is the waiting that is hardest."

"Months ago I was studying Asian history at Berkeley, now I am going to make history." Lisa slowly shook her head. "I won't lie to you, Huei Fun. I am scared."

"You *should* be. Just remember, you might feel all alone, but you are not on your own. Not even in Pyongyang."

"What if I am followed to Pak Chul's apartment building?"

"Assume that you *are* followed. Remember, you won't have a smartphone with a map of the city stored in it. Take advantage of a city tour offered by your official guide to learn the layout. Now I want you to practice your approach, as if I am your target. Explain your presence to me like I am Pak Chul, start the interview and, next, have a coughing fit, some excuse to go for a glass of water. Then get close, front or behind...and be flexible about your position. Strike, poke, insert. At his apartment in Pyongyang you will then clean up and leave. You will be met at the ground floor."

So that's what they did for half-an-hour, using unaltered pens similar to the modified instruments, but bought from a nearby stationary shop, until Huei Fun was satisfied. "Take a short break, drink some tea. We will go over counter-surveillance techniques until it is midnight, then sleep. Big day tomorrow."

Lisa rinsed her eyes in cold water, fortified herself with more cups of fermented black tea—called by the Chinese for its after-brewed color, "red tea"—and announced that she was ready for the next lesson.

Her trainer paced the living room. "No time to perform surveillance on others. Besides, it takes years to perfect the craft. Since you'll be on the receiving end, stay aware of your surroundings and anything or anyone that appears unusual. Frankly, Pyongyang will be like landing on another planet, so much so that every little thing will seem strange. Keep at it and your observations will adjust to what is considered normal there, enabling you to spot elements that seem out of place. Don't force it, Lisa. Let the impressions come to you and your mind will filter out the ordinary, leaving the unexplained. Look around as a newcomer would anywhere in the world. Don't hide your curiosity and don't flaunt it."

"When I've gone off on my own, the second day, how can I spot someone tailing me?"

"Here's the deal. If the watchers are professionals and not just run-of-the-mill citizen-spies common to North Korea...well, you *won't* spot them." Huei Fun stopped, folded her open palms together, as in prayer. "North Korea's state security operatives are very, very good at their job. On their territory you are at their mercy and hoping for a big dose of luck, some unexpected slip-up on their part. See, after 70 years of totalitarianism, there aren't many places to hide north of the DMZ. You will try to escape and they will probably track you down."

"Still trying to talk me out of it?"

"I won't sugar-coat the risks, Jin Sun. It is the original Hermit Kingdom, the most secretive and repressive society on earth. I would not volunteer for this mission," Lisa said solemnly and got up from her chair, rubbed the back of her neck. "Okay, let's get back to trying to spot followers. Some practices are shared whether in Asia or Europe. For example, the watcher will want to stay in the background, not attract attention by smoking a cigarette and tossing the butt on a sidewalk. In Pyongyang, it won't be the smoking that stands out—they smoke as much as in China—it'll be the littering, which is anti-social behavior. Street-sweepers keep their capital the cleanest city on earth. With that in mind, let's say you notice a man across the street raising his wrist to his mouth. What is he doing?"

"Biting off a hanging thread?"

Huei Fun laughed, in spite of herself. "Talking into a microphone secured to his wrist. He's speaking with another watcher who will take up the observation role now that you have noticed his colleague. You're being passed on. They'll want to maintain 'eyeball' contact. Next, if you walk fast or even jog, you have created a problem for yourself. People tend to notice someone hustling along, especially in a regimented society like in North Korea. Citizens are overworked six days a week and are too tired to move quickly. In addition, they'll walk at a pace similar to everyone else's in order to keep from being singled-out. If you go faster, *you* will stand out, but you won't lose your tail. You'll simply be passed on to another watcher working in a team."

"No point in running?"

Huei Fun said, "Only if your life is at stake. Again, if you are walking away from a watcher fast enough, another will pick you up and, in the process, leap-frog the exposed watcher. Now you're in the dark again. Make it easier on yourself and just assume that you are always under surveillance."

She stopped pacing next to the table, turned to look directly at her student. "The opposition will want to ascertain if *you* have people covering *your* back, as unlikely as that may be on their territory. Call it a choke-point. It could be a narrow bridge, a subway, an alley empty of dumpsters or vehicles. It's a place where other watchers can easily be picked out, people who don't naturally fit into that landscape. It is very effective."

"You mean, they will suspect I am not operating alone?"

"If they suspect you at all, they will find it hard to believe you hope to accomplish anything all by yourself. That's only logical. So, yes, they will be intensely curious to know who is helping you. One of their own or another foreigner? They will have standing orders to hold back until they have identified the other player." She drummed her fingertips on the table. "Here's the difference between surveillance in Seoul and in Pyongyang. In the south, there are cars, taxis, trucks and motorcycles on every road, with frequent traffic tie-ups. As a result, surveillance operatives will employ several vehicles. Three or four cars or motorcycles or scooters to box-in a walking suspect. The team coordinates by radio or phones and at any time one agent might 'leap-frog' another to seamlessly continue the observation. For an amateur like you, it will be almost impossible to spot. In North Korea, however, so few ordinary citizens have access to personal motorized transport, there is little point in using that technique. As you will see, there are broad, open avenues which are nearly empty, day or night. Can you imagine a policeman in Pyongyang writing out a ticket for what the Americans call 'jaywalking?' There is no rush hour traffic in Pyongyang. Only during organized parades around Kim Il-Sung square are there large numbers of people and vehicles. What I'm saying is, don't expect surveillance from a vehicle."

"How do I slip away from my hotel or the group in the evening, day after tomorrow?"

"Besides waiting for darkness and climbing down a hotel's fire escape? I'd suggest playing along with their system until it is inconvenient."

"A practical example?" Lisa prompted.

"If it was me, I would schedule a night out with some of the others in your group, a farewell dinner at a restaurant not far from the target's apartment. Your guide *has* to come. So tell the guide your plan on the morning of the second day. He is overworked and won't be thrilled with extra late night duty, but he is obligated to attend the dinner. Now, to sweeten the pot, you're picking up the tab for the drinks and entertainment. Unfortunately, it's not easy to find the right place in downtown Pyongyang—it poses no threat to Macau or even Seoul for nightlife—but there are a few restaurants you can go to. I'll give you a short list. Remember, no taxi will be available to drive you close to Pak Chul's. You'll have to walk, so practice what I've told you about watchers. The tell-tale sign of a cigarette glowing should be warning enough."

"So the hardest part of this affair might be getting free of the group, unseen."

Huei Fun nodded. "Walking out of a restaurant or club alone is sure to be noticed. Though darkness will be your friend, you must move fast and unobtrusively. That's a tall order in Pyongyang. I can only wish you the best of luck."

"You can pray for me."

Huei Fun shook her head. "Wasted words, I'm afraid. I am not a believer."

"No prayer is ever wasted."

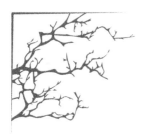

Chapter 15

THE MORNING SOUNDS of plumbing woke Lisa. Dawn's first light had barely passed through the tiny bedroom window from the alley in back. She heard the metallic jostling of bicycles, the steady honking of horns by taxis and small delivery vans. Time to get up, she thought, and climbed out of the bed generously loaned by her hostess who had fallen asleep on the sofa, curled up under a quilted comforter.

After using the bathroom, Lisa dressed for the journey in clothing provided. Gazing into a long mirror, she hardly recognized herself. The outfit featured a dark blue skirt falling just below the knees, and a matching jacket with wide lapels. Not a dreaded Mao suit, to be sure; nonetheless, it resembled a fashion statement from the 1960s. Huei Fun had insisted that that was how working women in Pyongyang dressed for office jobs. Better to fit in than stand out.

At least the jacket could be worn open, with a light blue blouse underneath, and the nylons fit snugly. The shoes were leather, black rubber-sole pumps...which *might* help her outrun someone. The purse was of smooth brown leather, a large one with shoulder straps. Actually, Lisa insisted, the clothing was not really as drab as most women's wear in North Korea, which would've looked strange on a young businesswoman arriving from prosperous China. Altogether, her hostess said, a cut above the plain light brown or pink business wear common in Pyongyang. The real purpose was to enable her to blend in on the second night, not appear so much like a foreigner.

Later, with a herringbone-weave carry-on bag, and wearing a pair of gold-framed glasses (lightly-tinted glass lenses, zero prescription) like the ones in Huei Fun's passport photo, Lisa and her China-based agent went to the hotel which the travel agency operated out of. Alone, she entered the international-class establishment, went to the agency's office and collected the passport and visa. She was told to meet her group at the airport in one hour, take a taxi. Back on the street, she saw Huei Fun half a block away and, as Lisa had hailed a passing taxi, her new friend's hands come up together in the universal sign of prayer. That simple movement managed to calm her rapidly-beating heart.

The formalities at Beijing's international airport passed in a blur, her introductions to the others traveling in her group—five men, two women, all citizens of the People's Republic of China—went smoothly. While they seemed surprised at her youth, her explanation that "the boss" had gone to Hong Kong for surgery evidently satisfied them. Her story was conveniently overheard by a representative of the travel agency used by North Korea and would, no doubt, be passed along to the North Korean embassy in Beijing. The excuse was verifiable. The firm's managing director really had flown to the ex-British colony for medical treatment, though the surgery was elective in nature.

On the Koryo Air flight, Lisa tried to study her company's promotional materials, avoiding conversation with the woman sitting next to her in the aisle seat. Her mind went back over Huei Fun's final words. Basically, she had been told that her mission was essential because of the rising tensions on the Korean peninsula, the threats of war going back and forth between Pyongyang and Washington. Although North Korea's leaders—three generations of the Kim family—found it convenient to publicly blame the United States for all of its problems and to bang the drums of war now and then, the presence of thousands of American troops on their southern border was not the regime's worst nightmare. For North Korea, the hatred of the USA was genuine and historically based...the Yankees' intervention to oppose Kim Il-Sung's attempt to conquer the peninsula under his brand of socialism over half a century ago. But any Korean, north or south, considered Japan the real bogeyman.

The Land of the Rising Sun's occupation of the Korean peninsula in the first half of the 20th century was still within the memory of many living Koreans, the insults to their people and land too strong to forgive. The stationing of U. S. troops in South Korea, as in Japan, was a guarantee that the indignities suffered at the hands of the Japanese Army and civilian government would not be repeated.

North Korea's closest ally, China, had also experienced the national humiliation of foreign occupation, beginning in the middle of the 19th century when Great Britain had forced opium grown in its colonial possession, India, onto the Emperor and people of China, opening up the Middle Kingdom to England's profitable and officially-sanctioned drug trade. Then came the French, Russians, Germans and Americans, all anxious to carve out areas of special interest in China.

Finally, while the land of the Mandarins was engaged in a civil war between Mao's communist forces and Chiang Kai-shek's Nationalist and embarrassingly corrupt government and army, the Japanese Imperial Army marched into north China's Manchuria. So began a brutal ten year occupation of China by Japanese forces. It could, realistically, be said that North Korea functioned as a kind of buffer state, situated between the two ancient Asian powers, China and Japan.

In conclusion, Khoo Huei Fun had alluded to cooperation and the exchange of information with America's CIA. Certain American politicians were sounding a clear warning of the danger to the United States if the North Koreans succeeded in developing an intercontinental ballistic missile (ICBM) delivery system, in addition to downsizing nuclear warheads. In that case, the day of reckoning would play out on American soil, not just in a faraway Asian land. The result, in the near future, could easily escalate from "saber-rattling" and bluffing to the real thing. The summit in Singapore was a hopeful sign, but one of unfulfilled promise at this point.

The undeniable fact was that nuclear war would mean the end of American democracy, replaced by marshal law. The military would rule

over a vast scene of wholesale destruction, cities with unbelievable loss-
es of human lives and physical degradation caused by fearsome, super-
heated explosions that preceded the mushroom clouds of atomic blasts.
There would also be the lingering effects of fallout, radioactive elements carried on the wind and in the rain. The major population cen-
ters would resemble the sets of Hollywood's most apocalyptic films, the
chaos that would follow such an attack bringing the richest country on
Earth down to a state of dystopia.

Lisa questioned, "Why are we going after Pak Chul now? Won't
it only heighten the sense of hatred and distrust, bringing us closer to
war?"

Huei Fun's reply: "Call it a reality check for the Kim family. Do
they really want to risk their wealth— billions of dollars hidden in
Swiss and Cayman Island bank accounts—and their hold on power in
a war they cannot win? If Kim Jong-Un is crazy—a term used too often
outside of a mental hospital to describe what seems like odd, inexplic-
able behavior—then armed conflict is inevitable. After all, his grandfather ordered the invasion of South Korea in 1950, so the Kim family
can certainly do it again. But we must hope that Kim Jong-Un will not
decide to bring down his kingdom along with him, as the European,
Adolf Hitler, was intent on doing to Germany at the end of WWII."

"What I am doing is important for peace?"

"Strange as it may seem, your mission may be our last chance." Huei
Fun had sighed. "We are not fortune-tellers. We do what we can, according to our best information and decision-making, and hope for a
good outcome."

Lisa's recollections were interrupted as the aircraft began its final
descent to Pyongyang's Sunan International Airport, located 15 miles
north of the capital. After a bumpy landing, the group was met by their
guide, a middle-aged man who introduced himself as Kim Chong Ho.
The latter names, he explained, came from the proximity of his birth-
place at Siniuju on the Yalu River, opposite the northern Chinese city

of Dandong, the site of most imports and exports between the two countries. His Mandarin, as a result, was excellent. He had been an official guide for twenty years and hoped that his esteemed guests would follow his recommendations carefully, to the benefit of all.

Mr. Kim was fuller in figure than other North Koreans in the airport, the rationing of food applying to most classes in North Korea's workers' paradise except for the privileged "core" class, the top military and government officials. After bowing and introductions had been concluded and customs cleared, the group piled into a minibus. Mr. Kim sat behind the driver and, through a microphone, announced that a short tour of the North Korean capital would precede arrival at their hotel. Business negotiations would be the priority tomorrow.

Amongst the group there was some confusion regarding the use of private cell phones. Many had heard that they would have to leave their smartphones at the airport. The travel agency in Beijing had been vague about that regulation. Mr. Kim assured them that phones were now allowed, though the situation was, admittedly, fluid. As for cameras, including those on their phones, care must be taken before snapping a photo. Best to clear that with their guide first. As a rule, no pictures of military installations or personnel, Kim advised. In fact, best not to take photos of any government buildings. As a matter of fact, don't snap any pictures without checking with your guide. Furthermore, group visitors should limit conversations with North Korean citizens, outside of their planned meetings, to the weather.

Then their guide rose up from his seat, faced the tour group. "On behalf of the People's Republic of Korea, welcome you to our socialist country. I am at your service during the entire time of your stay in our capital. It is my responsibility to see that your every need is seen to, that you enjoy a comfortable stay in our country. Please remain with the group at all times. It is not permissible to view the sights of the city on your own, unaccompanied. In the hotel, you are free to move about without me. But, I ask of you, refrain from venturing outside without me. There are security rules in place for the benefit of all citizens and visitors that will ensure a safe and productive visit. Thank you very much for your cooperation." The mandatory speech over, Kim sat down again and lit the first of many cigarettes.

Lisa, now known as Khoo Huei Fun, citizen and businesswoman from China, gazed out the windows and was immediately struck by the absence of other vehicles on the highway from the airport. Come to think of it, theirs had been the only aircraft on the runway. And the terminal building had been totally quiet, the only people visible were airport workers, customs and immigration officials, a few uniformed policemen and...no passengers at the departure counter. As for traffic, it was as if a drastic shortage of gasoline had hit the country—closer to the truth, there was a shortage of funds to buy vehicles. Their minibus was alone on the lanes leading into the capital. Set into the hillsides were large Korean characters extolling the regime in blatant propaganda. She was reminded of her view of the sign "Hollywood" on a dry hill in the Los Angeles area when she had flown out of the U.S. from LAX.

On entering the capital, her main impression was that it resembled a ghost city, the drab office blocks reminiscent of black-and-white photographs she had seen in books on East Berlin. It was like riding in a time machine back to the 1950s.

Even the clothing worn by young women walking on mostly empty sidewalks bore the distinctive stamp of uniformity, similar to her unstylish outfit. Pink or gray or light brown were the most vibrant colors worn by office workers. The men wore a kind of civilian uniform of long, baggy trousers and a tunic of matching color, usually brown
. The only touch of bright color came from an enamel pin worn above the left breast—what her Beijing contact had laughingly called the North Korean equivalent of the obligatory American flag lapel pin worn by U. S. politicians to demonstrate their patriotism since the September 11th terrorist attacks. In Pyongyang, the pin displayed the face of Kim Il-Sung, the country's "eternal president."

As for physical features, while many of the women appeared to have some "meat-on-their-bones," the men, without noticeable exception, were thin, almost gaunt. Clearly the North Korean economy was unable to provide adequate nutrition for most of the people. Only the ruling class enjoyed meals with lots of calories and, as a result, looked "well-rounded" like their leader, Kim Jong-Un.

Arriving in the capital with its largely hidden population of 3 million, Lisa easily spotted the city's incredible landmark for the modern age, a pyramidal tower of gleaming blue glass panels reaching skyward to a sharp point, over twice as tall as any other skyscraper in Pyongyang. The panels at the side, on the lower floors, combined with the structure's prominent centerline gave the building the appearance of a huge rocket, about to blast off into the heavens—a Tower of Babel for the 21st century or an architect's vision of a larger-than-life reproduction of Buck Rogers's intergalactic spaceship. That the capital's entire skyline contained, from her limited vantage, only three dozen modern skyscrapers—including what appeared to be recently-built, tall apartment buildings—relegated the unfinished monument designed as a luxury hotel, to a grand and eccentric extravagance for one of the poorest nations on earth.

Their guide had risen and proudly pointed out the sights on the min-tour of North Korea's premier urban center. Much time was spent in the vicinity of the Taedong River, the capital's largest waterway. As with the almost empty roads—Lisa counted seven vehicles in a single two-mile stretch—the wide river carried little traffic other than an old steamship, probably used for sightseeing tours. The minibus stopped in the vast Kim Il-Sung square, close to the river. Following an architectural pattern, each uninspiring government building was four to six stories tall, built around a central courtyard. They were monumental structures seemingly lifted straight out of Stalin's Moscow and lowered into place in the North Korean capital. Massive billboards atop the depressingly-similar buildings and long banners down the sides provided color to the otherwise boring grayness of official Pyongyang. The red, white and blue of the North Korean flag and its red star fixed within a white circle, were the most commonly-seen decorations.

Even though her travel companions tried to show polite interest, the overall effect on the group was probably like that of Mao's Red Guards rampaging through Beijing in 1967, enforcing uniformity in dress and attitudes on a silently suffering populace who mainly wanted to make a decent living and provide the essentials for their families, regardless of what ideology ruled the land. Maybe the guide sensed their lack of enthusiasm for his country's showplace. Kim Chong Ho directed the minibus' driver to head for the hotel, one selected by the travel agency. Hungry and tired, Lisa almost got up from her bench seat and cheered at the change in destination.

Instead, she sat quietly, determined to impress the guide with her dependable conformity to the group, even as she mentally stored away the lay of the land.

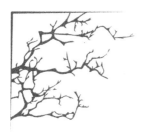

Chapter 16

THE EVENING WAS FORGETTABLE, an uninspiring dinner with a lifeless official from the Ministry of something-or-other giving a speech extolling the Kim regime and the benefits of their socialist system. After several toasts of inferior liquor, the official left and her group got up and drifted to their rooms. The next day started with the same gray skies as the day before, reinforcing her personal sense of "losing-the-will-to-live." She almost envied their guide the boost he got from nicotine, as he chain-smoked his way through the hotel's sumptuous breakfast of boiled egg, rice and watery orange juice. As Lisa ate a piece of toast she forced herself to concentrate on her presumed duties; that is to say, selling her company's planned joint-venture with the North Korean government. Best not to think of tonight's activity, she thought, and felt the two lethal pens in her inside jacket pocket.

But the more she tried to turn her mind to other things, the more she found herself brooding over the idea of executing someone. It wasn't so much the details or the unknowns she faced, it was the morality of killing a man, someone she had never met. Although she hated what Pak Chul had done many years ago—and there was no statute of limitation on murder—she did not actually hate the man himself. It wasn't in her nature to feel that way, and the closer she got to the moment, the more she questioned her apparently impulsive decision to take on the mission. After all, she was a college student, not a professional killer. Did other, more seasoned, operatives experience these doubts? she wondered.

With only fresh underclothes to distinguish her from yesterday's outfit, Lisa stood outside the twin-towered hotel favored by foreign visitors, leafing through her product brochures while waiting to board the minibus. Checking his wristwatch, the guide looked around impatiently for the two other ladies in the group from Beijing.

"Huei Fun!" a woman called from beside an old Mercedes sedan, that party's official guide leaning on it, "Khoo Huei Fun! What are you doing here?"

Startled, Lisa glanced up from her papers. She tried to compose herself and assess the situation. Act natural, she told herself, and waved. "Fancy meeting you here. How are you?"

The woman came near, under the careful scrutiny of both guides. "You left Shanghai in such a hurry, we all wondered what happened. Were the police chasing you?" she asked, laughing at her little joke.

Lisa shook her head. "Called away on urgent business in the capital," she explained, hoping the lie would pass muster. Was this woman a friend or a business associate, she asked herself, and settled on the latter. "You're in Pyongyang on business, too?"

"Why else would anyone come to North Korea?" the woman said, still laughing.

The guides were now paying close attention to the unexpected exchange. They were not smiling.

Lisa felt the world closing in on her. Time to cut things short. "Excuse me, I need more time to prepare my presentation. It's good to see you again."

"Khoo Huei Fun, have you forgotten my name? We worked closely together many times in Shanghai in spite of being with rival firms." The woman started to turn away. "Fine then, I see how it is. You were not sincere."

Lisa looked at her guide and shrugged. "I meant no offense, but we were never close," she told Mr. Kim, and got on the minibus. Sitting at the back, she winced at her feeble attempt to explain the encounter in this land of innate suspicion, where every meeting was planned out, nothing happened by chance.

On the road to the office of the ministry concerned with economic development, the first of the day's showers came down. Inside the government office, meeting with three North Korean officials, Lisa felt the oppressive spirit of the place. For a business conference, the room seemed too small and smelled of floor wax, pencil and eraser shavings. The government workers were all dressed in the same dark brown business suits and ties that they had probably worn on these occasions for the last twenty years. Indeed, the men facing her were all at least twice her age. Only one of them spoke Mandarin. He translated into Korean for the others. For Lisa, it became a surreal experience since she was assumed to be ignorant of the Korean language. Finally the morning, and endless cups of tea, was over.

Outside, the rain paused long enough for the visiting Chinese group to file back into the bus for the short drive to a local restaurant. As if sensing the mood of the group, Mr. Kim had arranged for lunch at a place located beside the Taedong River. Favored by Pyongyang's residents, Lisa learned that few groups of outsiders were brought here. The Chinese greatly enjoyed the chef's famous cold noodles and their spirits visibly rose. That's when Lisa took her guide aside and brought up a special request; that is, she, on behalf of her company, would like to treat the group to dinner and drinks at the Pyulmori restaurant (as suggested by Huei Fun). The coffee shop had a relatively well-stocked bar and was also known as a place where foreigners in Pyongyang often went. Her guide hesitated. Notice should have been given 24 hours ago, he maintained; however, he gave in and agreed. She almost felt bad for him. It was simply an additional duty taken on, not a time of celebration for the guide.

After lunch, it was back to the ministry and more discussions. It was still too early for any negotiations over areas of responsibility, percentage of profits, location of a manufacturing facility, and so on. A fast learner, Lisa basically faked it, doing her best to talk the language of business with frequent mention of 'raw materials' and 'products' and 'units' and 'profit/loss.' By mid-afternoon she was thoroughly bored. The meeting became an exercise in how to stay awake as the talk turned to levels of risk, projected number of workers required and their training. Even the issue of housing for the Chinese company's on-site manager was spoken-of.

Since none of the officials used laptops or tablets, Lisa made a wild guess that the discussion was being recorded. There was a lone secretary taking notes on a spiral notebook, sitting beside an old-fashioned black telephone. Not for the first time, Lisa felt she'd been transported backward into the 20th century. Very strange.

Blissfully, the business part of the trip came to an end. There were bows, hands shaken but, as yet, no deal. In the meantime, Lisa—aka Khoo Huei Fun—would return to Beijing, she explained, and present details to her company's executive staff. Then it was back to the minibus and a return to the hotel. Three hours before the scheduled dinner. The members of the group were, in effect, confined to the hotel.

Lisa showered and changed clothes. Out of the frumpy outfit and into a light-gray pants suit. After filing her nails, applying a bit of pink polish, she looked for something interesting to read. A search of the room revealed nothing. No Gideon's Bible in a Pyongyang hotel, no popular magazines. Well, there was a day-old newspaper with a picture of Kim Jong-Un in his usual uniform and *unusual* haircut, standing on a dais, reviewing stiffly-marching soldiers and happily observing old army trucks towing artillery pieces. The young leader was smiling and waving to the brainwashed citizens of his country in the square, a kind of civil blessing for his loyal comrades.

Her double in Beijing had been right, Lisa realized. It *was* the waiting that was particularly hard.

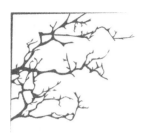

Chapter 17

THE RESTAURANT WAS lively, in sharp contrast to the rest of the capital of North Korea. The dining room was filled with loud conversations, the sound of utensils on bowls and plates, glasses clinking in toasts and a fascinating mix of languages spoken—Russian, Hindi, German and English, in addition to Chinese and Korean. Her temporary colleagues had put on different suits or dresses, and along with the change of clothing, their demeanor was less restrained than during the business day. The alcoholic drinks were taking an effect at their two tables. Their guide, Mr. Kim, restricted his consumption to tea.

Heavy rain drummed on the roof, but the noise of the storm was largely drowned out by talk and music. The food was tasty, though hardly the main attraction. It was, rather, the greater sense of freedom felt by the Chinese amongst the other foreigners. The light-hearted atmosphere reminded Lisa of a 1970s movie she'd seen on TV, *The Poseidon Adventure,* where cruise-goers had partied in style while the sea was working itself up into a giant wave that would soon turn their ship upside-down. She slowly sipped a glass of red wine, determined to maintain a clear head, and carefully scanned the main dining room. The location of the woman's bathroom was of particular interest, always an acceptable excuse to slip away from the group and the guide.

"I have to use the restroom," Lisa told the guide. As he started to get up, she pointed across the dining room, adding, "It's just over there. I'll be right back."

When she reached the ladies' lounge, a party of five entered the restaurant and immediately joined diners at a large round table. Greetings and drinks were exchanged in German and one of the diners grabbed a pretty Korean waitress and insisted she sing along with them. Lisa seized the opportunity, draped a white towel over an arm, lifted a round tray of used plates and glasses and, raising it to face level, bused the dirty dishes through the kitchen and into the dishwasher's room. She kept on going out the back door, saying in Korean, "Smoke break."

A green bamboo umbrella was set next to the door. She took it and entered an alley. Twilight was passing into evening and she glanced around, searching for the tell-tale sign of a glowing cigarette. Surely a nightspot frequented by Pyongyang's small expatriate community would be under observation, she thought. Perhaps it was the combination of night and the rainstorm, but she did not spot any watchers and felt more confident. Anyway, she told herself, she had to leave the immediate vicinity since her guide would soon grow restless, suspicious of any prolonged absence.

The tall, modern-looking apartment building she sought was only a few hundred yards from the restaurant, just as her Beijing contact had described. It was not far from Pyongyang's so-called 'Forbidden City,' a residential compound for top Party and military people and their families. As a result, the apartments' balconies and windows faced south, away from the housing of the privileged class. Entering the building, she left the umbrella at the door and followed a young couple into the lobby. They looked back over their shoulders at her on their way to the elevator.

Lisa scanned the ground floor. No concierge was on duty, or else he was busy in another part of the building. She opened the door to the stairs and climbed up to the fourth floor. In the hallway she spotted a thin, elderly man wearing the typical civilian uniform of tunic and trousers. He looked familiar. Then the elevator door opened—one of the benefits of living in a district close to the elite—and he was gone. Lisa made her way down the hall to the target's numbered door and knocked. No answer, so she rapped on the door again. There wasn't a sound from inside, just a few TVs on in other apartments.

"Hello," she said quietly, "I am a student assigned a project, to interview the heroic Pak Chul. May I speak to you, sir?"

Still no reply. She put an ear to the door. Suddenly it came to her...the man at the elevator. She turned and ran back down the hall to the stairs, recklessly taking them two at a time. She had no plan. She would have to improvise, she told herself, and left the stairwell. When she was halfway across the lobby and deep in thought, the front door swung open and a man in a black uniform entered the apartment building.

"Stop," he ordered. "Hold out your hands!"

A policeman, she realized. Her knees started to buckle. "I am a Chinese citizen. I became separated from my group," she said lamely.

"Show me identification!"

"I came in here to ask to use the telephone. I am lost. Can you help me?"

The policeman repeated, "Your passport."

"At the hotel. You know it is required to leave it there."

The policeman frowned. He reached for his radio to request instructions. Before he could talk, a dark figure came up behind and landed a one-handed blow to his neck. As the Pyongyang cop dropped to his knees and fell forward, the newcomer reached out, took Lisa's left arm and tugged her away from the body. Outside, he paused to look at her.

"You are Roh's agent?"

"Who are you?"

"Your ticket to freedom. Do exactly as I say and you *might* survive this night." The slender young man wore dark slacks, a black long-sleeve shirt and a charcoal gray sport coat, evening wear for one of North Korea's privileged class. He was taller than her, about six feet, and moved like an athlete. His hair was cut short. He possessed strong facial features, though in the Korean sense, there was nothing about him that made him stand out from the crowd...except for the clothes.

He switched from Korean to good, if accented, English. "I am your contact. Call me 'Eddie.'"

She nearly collapsed in his arms. "He got away. The target was leaving as I got to his floor. I have failed."

The man who called himself Eddie shook his head. "Pak Chul walked down the street to an open shop across the road. He does the same thing every night. Didn't they tell you?"

"No."

"We'll take my car." He indicated a compact four-door wagon, light blue, parked at the curb. "Run with me or you'll get soaked."

Inside the car, she asked, "The police officer...is he dead?"

"A concussion. He'll come to with a bad headache, maybe a broken nose from hitting the floor. Forget about him."

Eddie fired up the small engine, put it in gear and pulled away. The windshield wipers worked hard to clear the glass. As she studied him, her composure started to return. Somehow she felt she could trust this stranger. In addition, she knew that her life was in his hands.

"The cop can describe me."

"Without a name, it will take a bit of time. Your guide will be anxious by now and will call a superior for advice. Then a localized search will begin for you, as a Chinese citizen. After the cop recovers consciousness and talks, the authorities will make a connection and check the hotels. Within hours after we take out Pak Chul, the hunt for you will go national."

"Get him? But he's gone."

Eddie switched off his headlights. There were no other cars on the city street. "There, fifty yards in front, just stepping off the curb," he said, and accelerated. Ten yards away from the old man Eddie flicked the headlights back on and switched to high beam. The man known as Pak Chul froze like a deer caught in the blinding glare of the oncoming lights.

As the front bumper struck the ex-army officer, Pak Chul let go of a small paper bag and packs of cigarettes flew up and off the windshield. Thrown like a proverbial rag doll off the car's front end, he hit the unyielding trunk of a roadside tree. Even above the car's raucous engine, Lisa heard the sickening crunch of the man's damaged body as it slid down the trunk to the sidewalk.

Eddie stomped on the brakes, skidding the tires on the wet asphalt and shifted into reverse. Turning off the headlights again, he used the weak reverse lights to guide the vehicle backward until the right rear tire bumped up and over an object in the gutter. Smoothly, Eddie shifted back into first gear and drove forward, then increased speed as he moved up the gears until he rounded a corner. On the riverside road he set the lights on low beam and, opposite a small island, turned onto a bridge.

"Yanggak Island and bridge," he muttered, but not in explanation. It sounded more like a goodbye. "We are heading south, out of the capital. The roads are in good condition around the Pyongyang. We'll make good time."

"Where are we going?"

"Out of North Korea."

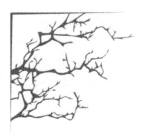

Chapter 18

NIGHT IN PYONGYANG.

They could have been on the dark side of the moon, she thought. Travelling away from the city center into the outlying districts, affected by an all-too-common power outage, worked in their favor. Eddie slowed down as they left the central area, trading time for the cloak of ordinariness. Of course, the presence of any private cars on the road at night was, in itself, an unusual sight in Pyongyang. It suggested that the driver and passengers belonged to the core class, or were members of a foreign government's mission or one of the international agencies in the country. A routine police stop was, therefore, not expected unless he was pulled over for excessive speed or suspicion of drunk driving.

Suddenly Lisa was shaking. Her arms and legs wouldn't stop moving. She felt tears, warm and wet, flowing down her cheeks. "I think you saved my life," she said softly, and wiped her cheeks.

"It's the shock, a delayed reaction to what just happened. It's natural. The main thing now is to stay alert. We're a long way from safety."

"You're coming out with me?"

"Can't stay here any longer. My cover is blown."

"So you work for Mr. Roh, too."

"Sort of. It's the same agency."

"How long have been in North Korea?"

He laughed, releasing some of the built-up tension.

She got the impression that Eddie didn't laugh much in Pyongyang. She tried again. "Where were you born?"

"Pyongyang."

"But...I thought you were one of us."

"I am Korean." He glanced at her. "Okay, Roh recruited me years ago, while I was a student at the university. I'd just completed active military service and he was on a delegation from South Korea during a temporary thaw in relations."

"Why did you risk it?"

"My parents were scientists, assigned to Kim Jong-Il's missile program. A medium-range missile, still under development, was rushed to a launch pad on orders from our Dear Leader. It exploded. My parents were killed."

"The regime executed them for the failure of the launch?"

"That is always a fear amongst scientific staff. No, it was the falling debris—hot, jagged metal—that hit them. The government lied to me about their their deaths. After completing my university studies I joined the Ministry for State Security. That's how I found out the truth."

She didn't mention that her government had also concealed the truth of a parent's death. "So you are like...a double agent?"

"Was. By morning a manhunt for me will be in full swing. You, too."

"I guess that makes us important," she said defiantly.

"It makes us dead, if they find us. Don't kid yourself, Khoo Huei Fun—"

"Lisa. Call me Lisa. My real name is—"

"I don't want to know your correct name. Nor will you know mine while north of the DMZ. If captured, they will torture us to extract information."

She fell silent then, the gravity of her situation resurfacing. Looking out, there were few signs of light in the buildings passed. Now and then she caught what must be the flicker of candles. Eddie had switched off the headlights and was driving only 45 miles per hour on the empty divided highway. He turned onto a cloverleaf directional ramp and she sensed they were no longer going south. She imagined that if she had a compass, the needle would point east.

"We left the Pyongyang-Kaesong highway south and are now on the Pyongyang-Wonsan road. It's roughly 130 miles to the east coast city, then another 70 miles south to the DMZ." He rubbed his eyes one at a time, eyes already weary from straining to drive without the lights on. Fortunately, the rain let up and the clouds parted enough to let a full moon illuminate the black ribbon of roadway. "I know how the authorities think. It'll take a few hours for them to put all the pieces together—Pak Chul's death, your disappearance and, by morning, my failure to report for duty.

"They will expect a dash to Kaesong and an attempt to enter the restricted industrial zone shared with South Korean businesses. Our security is vigilant at all entry points to the complex, knowing their counterparts in Seoul could use the manufacturing plants' transport vehicles to smuggle someone out. As for Pyongyang, checking the hotels in the capital won't take long. First thing in the morning, they will question the reps of foreign governments whether anyone has sought asylum in their embassies.

"Of course, the airport will be watched closely, though the few flights out per week make it a lower priority than the distribution of police might suggest. Then there is the railway, a trip of 6 hours northwest to the Chinese border. All coaches will be thoroughly searched, stations along the route monitored." He shrugged. "When the entire country is already an armed camp, the tightening of security is not all that noticeable to most citizens. We cannot expect help from anyone."

"Shouldn't we head west to the coast? Find a small boat, maybe a fishing vessel, and sail south from Korea Bay into the Yellow Sea?"

"That way *is* more direct than heading to the shores of the East Sea. And that is why we are taking the longer route. My *ex*-colleagues will not expect us to go all the way to Wonsan, the site of several military installations. Once Pak Chul's body and the street where he died is examined, investigators will know it was a homicide by vehicle, not just a hit-and-run committed by an inebriated and scared citizen. By mid-morning the police and security apparatus will have clamped down on *all* means of travel. Backing over him to make sure he was dead elevates the charges from vehicular manslaughter to a homicide." Eddie sighed noisily. "By now, the officer will have been discovered and taken to the hospital. The couple that entered the building before you must've called the authorities, reported the presence of a suspicious person. The cops will get your description from them, and that will match up with one provided by your official guide."

"You saw them?"

"And you, taking to the stairs. I was across the street in this car. When Pak Chul left, I knew you'd come down soon. The cop's arrival on foot didn't surprise me at all."

"So you knew those people would contact the police."

"In this country, everyone suspects the worst of other citizens. Children are taught in school that reporting on their parents is the right thing to do. Students are told that even looking unhappily at the omnipresent pictures of our esteemed leaders, Kim Il-Sung and Kim Jong-Il is a grave offense, and that is enough to condemn a parent."

As the road became less straight and rose in elevation, Eddie switched on the headlights and increased speed. "There are few police-men patrolling this highway. With so few private vehicles, what would be the point? That can work to our advantage. However, if we do en-counter a patrol they will try to pull us over."

"You can outrun them?"

"Not in this car. It's one of only two kinds made in this country. Al-though the government imported a thousand Volvo sedans, most were allotted to the elite of the Party and military. A few to the police. Prob-ably none are used on this road."

"It is your personal car?"

"No."

"How were you able to obtain it?"

"Borrowed it from my boss. I told him I was taking out a young lady. His wife got excited at the prospect of playing matchmaker. She convinced him to loan me the vehicle for the night." He patted the dash. "If I had taken an official car from the motor pool, we could listen in on police radio broadcasts. But," he sighed, "one cannot have everything."

"We should have taken the cop's radio."

"For use in the city, yes. Out here it would be useless."

Lisa opened her purse, took out her watch and saw that it was less than an hour to midnight. "How long until we reach the coast?"

"From here, maybe 3 ½ hours. The cover of darkness works both ways. Little traffic, but our lights can be spotted from a mile away. When helicopters join the search, it'll get more complicated. But that won't be for awhile."

"What is the condition of this road? Can we go faster?"

"The terrain is very rugged. With the harsh weather, the road surface suffers. We must cross the Nangnim Mountains, the main north-south range. Lots of elevation changes, tunnels, river valleys and switchbacks. This road is anything but straight."

"Eddie," she said, "what are our chances?"

He shrugged again. "Less than fifty-fifty. A *lot* less."

"Well, I am an optimist."

"Me? I am a realist."

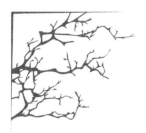

Chapter 19

EDDIE HAD NOT EXAGGERATED about the land. It became un-believably rough, the highway following a ridge with a steep drop-off on their side, which continued for many miles. Guard rails were a lux-ury not seen often. Lisa imagined lonely travelers going over the side, plunging down into narrow canyons, and lost for weeks in the rocks and scrub. The effects of a long day filled with soul-killing meetings with faceless bureaucrats, followed by the excitement of slipping away from the dinner party, the high suspense of entering the target's apart-ment building and the shock of finding Pak Chul gone, the policeman's intervention and Eddie's arrival and violent solution—running down the elderly murderer—and the high-octane tension of making their es-cape, had reached a crescendo of doubt and fear. Only her companion in flight gave her reason to hope. She closed her eyes.

"Keep your eyes open," he ordered. "You *must* stay alert."

"What is it, Eddie?"

"A police car. We are well past the town of Kangdong, nearing Yangdok, about fifty miles east of the capital. Ordinarily, only military vehicles in convoy would travel after dark. That means the alert has broadened in scope, and sooner than I'd hoped."

"They will turn around, come after us?"

"Watch the mirror. Let me know if you spot lights coming up be-hind us. I must concentrate on the road."

"Eddie, do you believe in God?"

He glanced at the rear-view mirror. "What kind of God would cre-ate a North Korea?"

"A false god."

"What are you saying?"

"He gave us life, He gave us land and the sea to support us. He did not make the government, Kim Il-Sung did. Kim fashioned an entire country for himself and taught the people to worship him as a god."

"You think *your* God will save us?"

"I cannot blame the Creator for our mistakes."

"Will He help us?" Eddie repeated.

"Have you driven this road before?"

Eddie snorted. "Even as a respected member of state security, there are limits to internal travel. Written authorization must be obtained to show up in Wonsan."

"How old are you?"

"Twenty-seven. Why?"

She was trying to formulate a reply when a pair of headlights appeared in her side mirror, steadily growing closer. "It might be the police."

"They are curious. They will hold back, unsure of us. According to their way of thinking, only citizens on official business, people of the privileged class, would be driving into the mountains at midnight. They won't want to risk offending a member of the Party elite." He rolled his neck in circles, working out the tension. "As they get a closer look at our vehicle, they will realize that no member of Pyongyang's ruling class would drive a small car like this one out of the capital. They will wait for a suitable place to pull us over."

"What can we do?"

"Bluff. You are the daughter of a Party leader attending one of Wonsan's many universities. As a security officer, I am taking you there."

"They will accept that?"

"Only if they are not in radio contact with their headquarters. It is better we choose a spot, set the terms." He slowed down and, shifting into neutral, coasted onto the dirt shoulder, an abrupt plunge into nothingness on the passenger side, a clump of stunted pine trees on a hill on the opposite side of the road. He left the parking lights on and let the engine idle.

The police car pulled up and parked ten yards back. Before the driver or his colleague opened their doors, Eddie threw his open, sprang from the car and walked up to the cruiser—a mid-size wagon/SUV that resembled a Mitsubishi Outlander but was made by North Korea's Pyeonghwa Motors. He held up his ID wallet. The driver tried to get out and Eddie kicked the door shut, pulled a handgun from a shoulder holster and aimed it at the startled cops.

"Take your hand off the radio transmitter." He pointed the muzzle at the uniformed cop in the passenger seat and told the driver, "Switch off the motor, turn off the lights, hand me the keys. Do everything slowly and carefully or I will shoot you. Do you understand?"

Both cops nodded grudgingly.

"Unholster your guns, hand them to me one a time." The cops, furious at their predicament, recognized their opponent's determination as well as the short barrel of the Model 70 pistol moving from one head to the other. One after the other, Eddie threw their guns over the roof of the police car and down the steep slope. He backed away a few feet. "Keep your hands where I can see them and get out of the car on the driver's side, both of you." After the cops had complied, he said, "Driver, handcuff your partner's hands behind his back and give me the key." With that accomplished, Eddie took the driver's cuffs and secured the second cop's hands behind his back, and threw both handcuff keys over the cliff.

Lisa remained in the car, watching the drama play out in the rearview mirror. Every few seconds she scanned the road ahead and back, in case another vehicle approached.

"Sit down and cross your legs," Eddie said, holding the pistol steady. The gun resembled the Russian-made Makarov or German Walther PPK, deadly at short range. The older of the pair, the driver, had more weight on him, and clumsily dropped down onto the pebble-strewn ground, landing awkwardly on his side. Eddie grabbed the man's tunic and tugged him into a seated position. The younger cop leaned back against the side of their cruiser and slid down off the sheet metal onto the dirt.

Eddie stepped around the unhappy cops and, using the ignition key, unlocked the trunk. Rummaging around, he found out a coil of rope, some rags and duct tape. Ordering the cops to get up, and again assisting the older guy, he marched them across the highway at gunpoint onto the wooded hillside. Minutes later he returned, closed the cruiser's trunk, got behind the wheel and started the engine.

As Lisa watched, Eddie backed up the cruiser onto the road and kept reversing for about a hundred yards. He spun the car around, facing it south, got out and, with hands on the A-pillar by the windshield, pushed the front wheels of the patrol car over the edge. A final shove from behind the vehicle sent it crashing down the steep slope into a ravine, visible to her only because, a moment later, the landscape was sharply illuminated by an explosion and the flash of orange flames. As silence descended once more, black smoke rose from the wreck and merged into the dark sky in the isolated region. Eddie appeared at the door of their car and climbed behind the steering wheel.

"Let's get out of here," he said, breathing heavily. As he pulled back onto the highway, he flicked on the headlights. "That will buy us some time, maybe enough to reach Wonsan and turn south."

"What did you do to them?"

"You mean, did I shoot them? I don't have a silencer, so you would've heard the shots." He ran a hand through his short hair. "They're not my enemies. They're just trying to do a job and stay alive in this cursed country." He looked at his passenger, gave her a quick, totally unexpected wink of his right eye. "I tied them to a stout tree, back to back. They are sitting comfortably, except for the chill of the night air. Their mouths are stuffed with rags and secured by tape. Compared to how we'd be treated in custody, they've got it good."

"I was afraid you would kill them."

"I have no such orders," he said sharply. "Pak Chul was different."

She lowered her head. "I'm sorry."

"Now is a good time to pray to your God. We have a long, winding road ahead and it is already one a.m. Four more hours with the cover of darkness. We'd better be close to the border by then."

Lisa shivered in the cold mountain air, rubbed her arms to stimulate warmth. The car's heater was broken, typical of North Korean products, she thought. Desperate to learn of any obstacles in the journey ahead, she sensed the burden on her new-found colleague. There were times when talking got in the way of understanding.

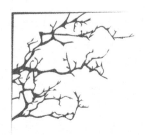

Chapter 20

THE NEXT SIXTY MILES passed uneventfully, the mountain town of Yangdok left far behind. Eddie drove without the use of headlamps. The highway followed a river bed before climbing again onto a ridge high above the valley. Crossing the Ryesong River, the blacktop turned northeast with a view of the darkened city of Koksan in the west. After passing through a series of tunnels engineers had blasted through the previously impassable mountains, the highway turned due east, hugging a river before entering another tunnel.

It was a land of high mountains, forests, and barren valleys in spite of rivers swollen with late spring snowmelt—a sparsely-inhabited land, perfect for two fugitives in a police state. The road was a treacherous and weather-damaged paved path of sharp curves and switchbacks barely visible until it rose up onto a plateau. Only then did the full moon enable them to see beyond the next sweeping turn. In the near distance Lisa saw snow on the higher peaks, then the highway turned northward.

About a mile further on Eddie switched on the lights as they entered a long dark tunnel. "Did you hear that?"

"No."

"The rotors of a helicopter, going east." He had slowed to ten miles an hour, peering into the blackness for that proverbial 'light at the end of the tunnel.' Nearing the source of the moonlight, he switched off the lights again and slowed to a stop. "We'll wait a few minutes for it to pass. Probably heading to Wonsan, an airport or a military landing field."

"Looking for us?"

"I don't know. No searchlight aimed at the road, so probably not."
He took a penlight from his jacket, shone it on the dash. "The gauge
shows the tank is over half empty. I wish we'd had time to siphon fuel
from the patrol car. Couldn't chance it though."

"There's enough to get us to the DMZ?" She tried to keep the
doubt and anxiety out of her voice.

"On a straight road, sure. But ours is filled with curves and elevation changes, which'll eat into gas mileage. Like I said, pray. It can't
hurt."

Five minutes later, they were just north of the late dictator Kim
Jong-Il's pet project, a ski resort at Masik Pass. Another tunnel and they
were heading northeast once more, close to the city of Wonsan, a port
located by the deep waters of the East Sea.

As Eddie skirted the city of over three hundred thousand and
turned south onto a secondary highway, she asked, "You seem familiar
with our route, yet you've never travelled it before."

"Google Earth," Eddie confessed. "As a trusted security officer, I
have access to the internet. Not a lot of unsupervised use, but I took advantage of every minute."

"No one was suspicious?"

"My excuse? Planning a holiday, my first ever to Kumgangsan in
the extreme southeast. I like to hike, and the mountains there contain
many waterfalls and mineral springs."

"You would go alone?"

"I do not have a wife."

"No girlfriend either?"

He rolled his neck again. "We should keep things professional,
don't you agree?"

"Sure, Eddie. I know when to be quiet."

Where the road south of Wonsan split into two routes—one leading into that mountainous wilderness of rocky crags, Buddhist temples

and monasteries that Eddie had mentioned, the other leading to the southwest and the borderlands—he pulled off the road.

He lifted up her purse, laid it on her lap. "Empty it. Pocket only the items you think you'll need for the next few hours, much of which will be on foot. Throw out the purse and what remains into the brush on the far side of the road."

"Nothing here that identifies me. My passport, as a citizen of the People's Republic of China, is at the hotel."

"Wrong. By now, the passport and your luggage will be at the Ministry of State Security. Nothing at all with your name on it?"

She reached inside her pants suit jacket and felt the two pens. There was also the folded letter of introduction to Pak Chul. She pulled it out and, with Eddie's penlight, examined it. In the small pile on her lap lay a small spiral notebook, meant for the fake interview with the target.

He pulled the notebook and paper out of her hands. "Tear the letter into little pieces. After we drive on, lower your window and scatter it to the wind and rain. Same thing with every page of the notebook, except the cover. That's of heavier stock and has the brand name of a South Korean company." He ripped off the cover, flicked a metal lighter and held the flame to it. When the flames reached his fingertips, he lowered the window and let the burned paper fall to the shoulder. "Is that everything?"

She kept a metal nail file and a compact. Opening the compact, she showed him the small round mirror. "For signaling once we're across?"

"Okay. Wait on the paper until we're moving again. Get rid of the rest."

After she had thrown the purse and various objects as far from the road as she could, Eddie pulled back onto the two lane blacktop. Overhead, clouds raced inland from the East Sea, driven by the monsoon winds. Within minutes on the poorly-maintained road south, raindrops pounded the roof and windows of their car. While the additional light from the moon was lost they gained a bit of security from the storm, the reduction in visibility cutting both ways. However, he had to drive more slowly because of potholes and bumps in the road surface, in addition to the heavy rain.

As far as Lisa could see, the land was planted with rice fields that led up to forested highlands. Then they were into a featureless countryside, hills and bare mountains, perhaps stunted bushes clinging to the smooth stone. Now and then she could pick out a massive boulder, otherwise very little detail emerged during the periodic breaks in the storm. The road went along a ridge, as in the Nangnim range, and traced a path southward with lots of sharp bends, sudden drops into valleys, and river crossings on narrow bridges.

Eventually, Lisa had to speak up, and not just for her benefit. She could see Eddie's eyelids drooping and his head snapping back as he fought for alertness. Falling asleep at the wheel would be disastrous in this country, still about 30 miles from their ultimate destination. Noisily she cleared her throat. They'd had nothing to eat or drink since leaving Pyongyang and her throat felt raw.

"Eddie, are you okay?"

"A cigarette," he tapped the small glove box, "something to keep me awake."

She found a pack, a Chinese brand, with a small box of wooden matches rubber-banded to the pack. She took one out, lit it and handed the unfiltered cigarette to him. "I didn't know you smoked. Most Korean men do."

"Only when necessary. Otherwise, I try to stay in shape."

"I have a question."

"Go ahead."

"Was Pak Chul the first person you have killed?" She coughed as the smoke from his cigarette drifted across her and caught in her throat. "What I mean is, have there been others."

"He was the first," Eddie said, and rolled down his window a crack.

"Why weren't you chosen to do the job in the first place?"

"I can only guess, Lisa. Probably Roh's people didn't want to risk exposing me as an agent. I was a 'sleeper,' not actively providing intelligence reports until recently."

"Then why involve you in my mission? That alone blew your cover."

He nodded wearily. "These decisions are made without consulting a field agent...in my case, a double agent. Maybe the Americans insisted on action. Lisa, I really don't know how it was decided, only that we are now on the run. A couple more hours and we lose the protection of night. Weather permitting, helicopters will be up in the sky, foot patrols along the length of the DMZ will be enhanced with orders to shoot on sight."

"I think Roh wanted to bring you in."

"Oh?"

"Yes," she said firmly. "He knew I was going to need an associate, someone strong. I'm no spy or intelligence operative, let alone an assassin. I know that now. He knew it when he sent me here."

"To draw me out?" Eddie took a long drag on the cigarette. "He picked a dramatic way of doing it."

"We are so close now, I'm sure we'll make it."

The final town of any size before the demilitarized zone was Pyongyang, a name similar to the capital city's, but a bland, truly depressing place. The storm had passed into the west and, far away, over the Sea of Japan, the first light of dawn appeared. The road surface had deteriorated further and the small car bounced and jostled on their southwesterly course. Suddenly the engine sputtered, the car slowed down and, the gauge on empty, rolled to a stop.

"Time to walk," Eddie said, and got out. He gathered a few items from behind the back seat—a folded tarp, tow rope with metal hook, a scissor jack.

Before, Lisa hadn't noticed the bulge under his left arm. Now she saw the butt of the handgun. How would a pistol protect them from the automatic rifles of the soldiers? she asked herself and climbed out.

Walking past the front of the car, she noticed the dented grille, bumper and hood, a reminder that the young man who had shown such daring and restraint on the highway with the policemen had also demonstrated quick-thinking and deadly aggression in Pyongyang.

The land to the south was forested, no trail evident. She stretched her arms once to limber up before following Eddie into the woods of pine, larch and spruce.

The DMZ beckoned.

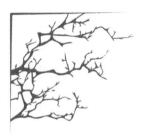

Chapter 21

LISA HAD NEVER FELT so tired in her life, which included over thirteen years of twenty-hour days of studies in school and in after-school study sessions, existing on four hours of sleep per night. It was necessary and important to push herself like that, for her parents' sake and for future opportunities. But this was different, a stark, unforgiving course in the academy of life and death. Her chances of survival, and Eddie's, a young man she felt very close to, might depend of their ability to hear the slightest metallic sound or gain a glimpse of shining metal through the tree cover.

"How close are we?"

"Two miles, maybe less."

"The DMZ is passable from this side?"

"It is a no man's land, 2 ½ miles wide. We face barbed wire fences, a concrete tank barrier, land mines remaining from the Korean War and watch towers. We don't have time to establish any pattern to foot patrols in this sector." He stopped and faced her. "Lisa, it will take one of your God's miracles for us to safely reach the other side."

"Inside the fences, the land is uninhabited," she said. "I have heard that wild animals are doing well without people bothering them."

"Too bad we're not bears or wolves. Come on, we've got to get there before daylight."

Hungry, thirsty and nearly exhausted, they trudged along at a pace set by Eddie, his longer legs striding forward toward the danger ahead, with the certainty of arrest, imprisonment and death at their backs. A few freestanding boulders offered some cover, as did the trees. Then they saw a wire fence, a strip of cleared land before it. By now the search for them would in earnest. Their sole advantage lay in the remote stretch of the border chosen for the crossing by Eddie. They were in a densely-forested part of the peninsula, a sector within the north-south Taebaek range that ran down the east coast into South Korea. They could see jagged limestone outcroppings against the southeastern sky. A wilderness area of forested mountains, it offered their best chance of escape...however slim.

She looked around. "I don't see anything. Do you see anything?"

He shrugged. "Run for the fence. And whatever happens, don't look back."

"Okay."

"Good luck." He squeezed her left hand.

She held onto his hand. "It takes a lot more than luck."

He pulled free. "Follow me," he said, and sprinted to the fence. After throwing the jack and tow rope over, he opened the tarp and covered the coils of barbed wire. She was right behind him when he turned. "Up you go."

The barbs poked through the tarp but she wasted no time climbing over the barrier, her shoes stepping on the horizontal wires between the posts. He went up after her and, sitting astride the top wire, tugged up the cheaply-made tarp, leaving pieces on the rusted barbs. After jumping down into the DMZ, he pulled off the tarp and rolled it up.

"Hope you had your tetanus shot recently," Lisa tried to joke. But her attempt at humor wasn't very funny inside the demilitarized zone.

He handed her the tarp and attached the heavy jack to the tow rope. "Walk a few paces behind me," Eddie said. He threw the jack ahead, as far as the rope allowed, then slowly drew the jack back, a primitive minesweeper. They advanced carefully up to the point where the thrown jack had landed and repeated the process, over and over. "It's a crude method at finding a path through a minefield, but it may keep us out of harm's way."

"If you say so."

"Without a metal detector, this is our only hope of triggering a mine before stepping on it. If we're unlucky and one detonates, we'll be injured by shrapnel and steel ball bearings but, hopefully, not fatally."

"That's your realistic side speaking."

But talking about their hazardous situation was pointless, she realized, and did as directed, cautiously looking over her shoulder despite his warning not to. They were alone, as far as she could see, the sound of wild birds their only company. It seemed like they'd spent hours moving through the heavy undergrowth in this lonely place. The sun was rising higher in the east, topping the coastal range, and sweat poured off her face even in the cool air of the mountains. Reckoning they were halfway across the forbidden land, they spotted the concrete wall, a tank barrier erected by Americans many years ago. Vines and creepers had taken hold in some spots, offering footholds.

At the wall, what North Koreans condemned as America's "Berlin Wall," Eddie waited, his chest heaving from the exertions of tossing the jack ahead and slowly drawing it backward. Laying down his jerry-rigged implement, he indicated to her the thick vines that offered a head start upward.

"I'll go first, check the ground below on the other side. I'll throw the tow rope and hook, minus the jack, over the wall to you. Stand back until it lands, then grab hold of it."

"Yes," she agreed and tried to smile encouragement.

In return, he patted her on the right shoulder before turning back to the wall and climbing up and over. Leaning off the top, he swung the jack along the ground, holding his breath. Removing the jack, he lowered the rope and, as soon as she got her hands on it, pulled her up. For a moment, they sat on top of the barrier together before dropping down onto the, presumably, friendly side of the DMZ. Then again, the entire width of the DMZ was a free fire zone, a place where no one had a right to be. Even on this side of the wall, a North Korean helicopter could hover overhead, raining down bullets or grenades.

The crossing to the fence on the south side of the zone was almost as agonizingly slow and uncertain as that from the north. Lisa felt weak from hunger and thirst. It was sheer determination not to give up or become a burden to the North Korean security officer known as 'Eddie' that she persevered. Amongst the thick undergrowth at the south fence, she allowed herself a sigh of relief. The safety of South Korean soil was but a few feet away. Eddie waited at the fence, having taken the tarp from her. He threw it over the strands of wire. After she had climbed over and stood, free in her homeland, he stooped down to reel in his improvised anti-mine device. The cry of some wild bird caught her attention a mere second before the blast erupted, knocking her off her feet. From the ground she saw her companion, sprawled and motionless inside the fence. As she rose up, ignoring any injuries she might have sustained, she saw spots of bright red blood on the back of Eddie's coat. She stumbled toward his body, a sob rising in her throat.

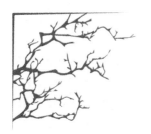

Chapter 22

"OH, EDDIE, NOT NOW," she cried. "We've come so far together."

She heard a low groan, saw his hands reaching down his right leg. Immediately, she climbed back over the fence and knelt down. Below the knee his trousers were hanging in strips, the leg still attached to the joint—a ragged wound of blood, ripped muscles and broken bones. She felt sick.

"Eddie, I know you're hurt," she choked out, "but you're going to make it. Do you hear me? You can't leave me here alone!"

He opened his eyes. "Climb mountains," he muttered, "I always wanted to summit a high mountain. Or be a K-pop star, making all the right moves." His mouth twisted as the pain raced up his spine to the brain, a delayed reaction to the trauma. His body was pumping out natural painkillers—just not enough to counter the severity of his wounds. He lifted his head, saw the mangled leg. "Use my handkerchief for a tourniquet, a stick to twist it tight. Loosen it every ten to fifteen minutes."

Lisa checked him over. She saw scattered bits of metal in the torn muscles, bits of cloth from his trousers lodged amongst the damaged tendons and ligaments—the embedded fabric bringing a serious risk of infection. No bright red blood was spurting. "Skip the tourniquet for now. The femoral artery was spared. You're suffering blood loss, but if we can get you to a hospital soon..." She left unsaid the obvious. If not death, there was the likelihood of amputation.

His eyes were glazing over. "Haven't got long before I succumb to shock. Find two short branches...rig a splint, knee to ankle. Use our handkerchiefs to secure the wood."

"I can do that."

"Wait. One more thing," He looked through the fence at the forested mountains, towering limestone crags punching skyward, the beautiful shape of Korean pine and cedar trees rising up the rocky slopes. He gulped the fresh mountain air, trying to focus his thoughts. "Before splinting, wrap a cloth tightly around the exposed muscle and bone, never mind if the fibula or tibia are broken. Seal it snug as you can."

With a nod, she pulled off her pants suit jacket and removed her white cotton blouse. She no longer felt the cold of the morning at the high elevation. Her breasts covered only by her brassiere, she tore the blouse in half, folded one piece around the wounds and, tearing the other half into two strips, tied off the cloth just below the knee and above the ankle. It didn't take long to find a pair of fallen branches suitable for splinting purposes. Within minutes she had him bandaged and up, bearing weight on his left leg. Using all of her remaining strength, mercifully augmented by a rush of adrenaline, she boosted him up and over the fence, his strong hands pulling upward while she bent down and put her shoulders into his backside. Finally, he was able to lower himself to the ground outside the fence. She saw a wince of pain distort his features as his left foot touched down, jarring his damaged body. The right leg dangled uselessly as he lowered himself onto the dirt and grass. They both knew he would soon slip into shock—a serious and natural condition for people and animals, protecting them from unnecessary suffering, but a state that could easily pass into unconsciousness and death. The alternative, without powerful narcotics, was that the awful pain of his wounds would torture him. Although they were now in South Korea, they were many miles from the nearest town with a clinic or hospital.

She climbed back over the fence, leaving the tarp, and sat beside him. "Eddie, we can't stay here. If I can find a suitable branch, I'll fashion a crutch."

He nodded, his eyes staring listlessly up to the blue sky, the first signs of shock appearing. "I'll be okay," he said softly. "Just give me a minute to rest."

She leaned over him, kissed his lips lightly, then went looking for a piece of wood that would function as a staff. She didn't have to search far. A branch of a Korean pine tree had fallen in a winter storm and was about the right length. Though not forked at one end for a shoulder support, the branch offered knotted handholds. She helped him up, put the makeshift crutch in his left hand and placed his right arm over her shoulders, providing support on his right side. The trail away from the DMZ was usually wide enough for them to walk side-by-side on the downhill path. Where it narrowed, they went sideways, her leading. It was very slow going, with sharp rocks and tree roots in the way, and no assurance of reaching help in time to save his leg. Many times Lisa just wanted to sit down and cry. It was the debt of freedom she owed to Eddie that kept her moving.

The mountain town of Chorwon was somewhere to the west, miles from their position. She was unaware of the dam on a river located closer to their present position, with personnel available to call for medical assistance. A city girl, she was new to the ways of the wilderness. Her body craved water, her throat ached and her lips were cracked. It had to be harder for Eddie with his wounds and loss of vital fluids. It seemed hopeless.

"Eddie, you've got to stay awake! I can't carry you, and I can't leave you and wander aimlessly." Lowering her companion onto a flat rock, she silently offered up a prayer for deliverance.

Suddenly, men in camouflaged fatigues appeared on the path, rifles held at the ready. A voice challenged, "We are a patrol of the ROK Army! Identify yourselves."

"We've come down from the north," Lisa answered weakly.

"Defectors?"

Too hard to explain. Instead, Lisa choked out the words, "Can't you see he is hurt? Please...he needs a doctor."

"We heard an explosion over an hour ago." The young sergeant let his submachine gun hang by its olive drab sling and came up to inspect the wounded man. "Medic!" he shouted.

Then Lisa dropped down onto the rock beside her friend and wept.

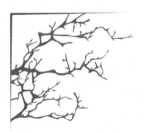

Chapter 23

THE FACE OF ROH HOVERED over her while she breathed in the aromas of antiseptics, room cleansing bleach and floor polish. There was also the scent of tobacco on his breath. Around her, the room was painted white, the nurses wore white, the doctors had on white lab coats. Behind the man known as Roh stood her mother, worry and wonder mixed in her beautiful brown eyes. At the first sight of her daughter's open eyes, her mother laughed for joy.

"Where am I?" Lisa said.

"Seoul National University Hospital," her case officer replied. "You are home and you are safe."

Her mother moved close, held her hand. "You kept calling a name. Who is Eddie?"

Lisa tried to sit up in the hospital bed, but slid down again. "Why can't I move?"

Roh pointed to the IV stand, the tube running into the back of her left hand. "Fatigue. Severe dehydration. A few days' rest and you will be okay."

"Eddie?" her mother prompted.

Lisa saw the nod from Roh. "He brought me out of the north, saved my life. Where is he?"

"Sorry," Roh told her mother, "she can't tell you much about the past two days. National security and so on. You understand?"

Mrs. Park held onto Jin Sun . "She is my only daughter."

"Eddie just left the operating room. The surgeon thinks the leg can be reconstructed," Roh explained, "though it will take many surgeries, a lengthy period of rehab. It is only fair to say that he owes *his* life to *you*."

A nurse entered the private room, took Lisa's vital signs and changed the IV bag. She turned to Roh. "Sir, I don't care if you are the Director of National Intelligence, you have five more minutes, then she must rest. Doctor's orders, not mine."

Roh bowed his head, though she was younger than him. "Thank you, nurse. It will be as you wish."

After the nurse had gone, Lisa asked, "When can I see Eddie?"

"Tomorrow," Roh said.

To her mother she said, "Please bring Heidi. I miss her very much."

"I don't think the nurse will approve," Mrs. Park said, before catching the look on Mr. Roh's face. "I will try to smuggle her into the hospital."

Roh turned and bowed to Mrs. Park. "And now, if you will allow me a private conference with your daughter?"

Lisa's mother leaned over the bed rail. "I love you, sweetheart," she told her daughter, kissed her forehead and left the room.

"Lisa, do you remember anything after the soldiers found you?"

She shook her head. "Tell me."

"Fortunately, they had a medic in the patrol. He helped you to sip water while placing salt tablets in your mouth." Roh went to the hallway, nodded to the armed guard, closed the door and returned to the bedside. "While the sergeant radioed for a medevac chopper, the medic removed Eddie's splint, unwrapped the bandage and cleaned out the wound as much as possible in the field. Then he applied sterile dressings to the leg. From what I was told, the army medic was very impressed with your first aid under such difficult circumstances. After the chopper found a landing site half-a-mile west, a crew went up to your position with canvas stretchers and carried you and Eddie down. IV's were begun inside the helicopter for the flight to this hospital. Eddie received plasma, in addition to a rehydration drip. It was a close thing, but with the doctor's expert care he won't lose his leg."

Lisa's eyes welled-up with tears. Quietly, she told the case officer about yesterday's experiences in Pyongyang, from the time of Khoo Huei Fun's Shanghai acquaintance appearing outside the hotel to Eddie's intervention at Pak Chul's apartment building and his role in killing the North Korean target. "If not for me, he would still be under-cover in Pyongyang and in good health."

"You can finish your story later," Roh said. "As for Eddie Lee..."

"Excuse me, is that his real name?"

"Is it important?"

"Maybe." A slight smile appeared on her tired face, breaking through the gravity of the informal debriefing. "Maybe it is."

Roh slid his hands along the raised bed rail to the foot of the bed. Staring at the monitoring machine, he said, "Information was trickling in about Eddie's situation in Pyongyang. Nothing specific, just hints that his position was no longer secure. Their security services are noto-riously suspicious, even of their own staff. After all, we play at the same game, trying to insert our people into their organizations as they seek to penetrate ours. Of course, a totalitarian system gives them an edge over a more open society." He shifted his gaze to her. "When a recent defector revealed details of intrigue in Pyongyang, a man fitting Eddie's description came up. In spite of his deep cover, I decided to pull him out."

"In the end, was it worth it?"

"You have avenged the murder of two American officers."

"Eddie did. I'll never know for sure if I could've used those pens."

"That's why Eddie was there last night," Roh admitted, "besides helping you to evade arrest. Lisa, you showed great courage and imag-ination under immense pressure. Never forget that you played a vital part in this mission. I'm proud of you."

"So that's it?"

"Should I remind you that you cannot speak to anyone of your recent...adventure?" The man known to her as Roh nodded, squeezed her hands and left the room.

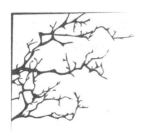

Chapter 24

SHE LAY HER HEAD BACK on the pillows and shut her eyes. At the sound of the door opening she came awake. The bedside clock indicated she had slept for almost an hour. Standing at the foot of her bed was a middle-aged man in a dark suit, a handsome though serious face.

"Excuse me for interrupting your needed rest, Park Jin Sun. My name is Moon...Mr. Moon." He leaned forward, held out an ID wallet which identified him as an officer with the KCIA. "We are relieved that you made it back safely. I would like to ask you a few questions?"

She shrugged her shoulders. "I don't understand. Surely Roh Dae-Jung has filed a report on the mission."

Moon shook his head. "I'm sorry, Miss Park, my agency does not employ anyone with that name."

"An alias?" she said weakly.

"One of many for that agent, I'm afraid."

"But he was just here, briefing me on the rescue."

Moon straightened up. "Ah, I am not too surprised. Your Mr. Roh has always displayed...moxie. Perhaps it was his way of taunting us."

"I am confused. He was my controller. He recruited me for the mission in Pyongyang."

"Miss Park, we would never send an amateur on such a dangerous assignment." Moon sighed and moved closer. "As Roh Dae-Jung, he set you up to enter his country and take part in the removal of one considered an embarrassment to the regime."

"Is this a joke?" she demanded.

"I am afraid not. Your Mr. Roh is an agent of the North Korean government's security services. As you have discovered, he is very good at what he does. In particular, his documents and identification papers are exceptionally authentic-looking, the work of an expert forger."

"You're telling me that my controller was impersonating a KCIA agent?"

"Clearly you are as intelligent as I was told." Moon attempted a smile but managed only to lose his frown.

"I...I don't believe it."

"He is very clever. We know of at least a dozen aliases he has operated under. Definitely a hard man to catch."

Lisa pushed herself up to a sitting position, challenged Moon with her eyes. "You know what I think?"

"No, Miss Park. Please explain yourself."

"You knew what Roh was up to and allowed it to happen. Tell me I am making this up."

Moon coughed, rubbed his chin. "I am not free to divulge details...but you are not entirely wrong."

"Our government saw it as a convenient way to strike back at Pak Chul and his son."

"Not exactly."

"What does that mean?" Lisa said accusingly. "Roh said that the son killed my father. The government lied about the death of Major Park."

Moon shook his head. "That is incorrect. Major Park was not the victim of a shootdown. The helicopter crash was due to a mechanical problem. Our leaders did not mislead you." Moon tapped his ID wallet on the bed rail. "You should believe me, Miss Park. We are sometimes accused of amoral activities, but deliberately lying to the daughter about the death of a brave soldier is not one of our faults. Face it, Roh played on your emotions. He's done it before."

"Why kill Pak Chul?"

"North Korea's Supreme Leader, Kim, is devious and ruthless. He is currently treading a narrow path politically over the negotiations with

the Americans over nuclear weapons. It is doubtful he will ever give up
all of his warheads and missiles. At the same time, he will not wish for
another public execution like when his half-brother was murdered in
Kuala Lumpur, Malaysia. It makes for bad PR." Moon stuffed the wallet
back in his coat pocket. "The new smiling, happy Kim apparently wanted a relic of the confrontational days of his grandfather 'disappeared.'
In Pyongyang, word is out that the people's hero, Pak Chul, was killed
in a traffic accident."

"In other words, I was used."

"The enemy may try to find you," Moon said, changing the subject.
"I am not confident we can protect you and your mother in Seoul."

"I guess not, if Roh can operate so freely here. What then?"

"Relocation." Moon folded his arms, came closer. "The Americans
now owe us. They will assist in obtaining new identities for your family.
Even the dog will have a new name and background."

Lisa raised her hands to her cheeks. "While in California I read of
their Federal Witness Protection Program. Is that what you mean?"

"Close. Not exactly the same thing, but close."

She shut her eyes, said softly, "I want to see Eddie again. I want to
help in his rehab."

"Eddie is going to America, too."

She opened her eyes, blinked. "Thank you for that."

"Don't thank me. Don't ever thank me, Lisa. You did what was
asked of you, believing it was for your country."

"You could have stopped me."

"Decisions were made at a level far above my office." He went to the
window and opened the blinds, revealing the skyscrapers of downtown
Seoul. "Your country will not know of your sacrifice, only a few at the
top have been told. So I say to you, on behalf of South Korea, please accept our gratitude."

She laid her hands on her chest, studied her broken fingernails.
"Will I be able to return to Berkeley?"

"Perhaps for your Ph.d. For now, a transfer to Harvard, Yale or Princeton can be facilitated. The East Coast of America...think of it as a change of pace. You will enjoy a full scholarship."

The nurse flung open the door, fixed her eyes on the visitor. "Your time is up, sir. You must let her rest now."

Moving to the doorway, Moon said over his shoulder, "I know we can count on your cooperation, Lisa."

"You mean my silence?"

"Think of a name and it is yours." At the door, Moon looked back and, finally, a reluctant smile broke through. "Goodbye and good luck."

The nurse went behind her patient, fluffed up the pillows. "Who is he? Your boss?"

Lisa shook her head. "He knows a man who said he knew my father."

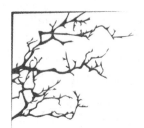

The End

Made in the USA
Monee, IL
11 October 2021

79830409R00073